ACKNOWLEDGEMENT

This fictional work is dedicated to the men and women who choose to provide for the safety and security needs of corporations, entertainment, and sporting venues and shopping malls throughout the United States.

Their reward is low pay and being demeaned, despised, and mocked. They are called "rent-a-cop", "mall cop", and "wannabees", yet they provide a service which public law enforcement lack both the resources and personnel to offer. Many of these men and women will transition into public safety service, but they all provide us with a safer and more enjoyable experience in our daily lives.

CHAPTER ONE

Melissa Gwen Harding was born in Lafollette, Tennessee, a small town just south of the Kentucky border. Her father was a pharmacist and her mother taught elementary school. She had a brother who is two years older and works as an auto mechanic.

From a very early age, Lissa (the nickname her parents called her) was enthralled with the red and blue beacons on law enforcement vehicles that drove up and down the streets of the town. She grew up as a tomboy playing baseball, basketball, and even football with her brother's friends. At ten she separated a shoulder trying to tackle one of her brother's buddies who went on to play high school and Division One college football at the University of Tennessee.

As a freshman in high school, she joined the Boy Scout Police Explorer program where she was given the opportunity to see the inside of how law enforcement operates. She got to see prisoners processed into the City Jail, do ride-a-longs with the cops, and see how the calls for service were received and dispatched.

Her first ride was with a female officer. Toni Wellbrock had five years on the job and enjoyed having the kids ride to learn what cops did and how they did it. Toni always gave the same instructions to the Explorers. She told them, "You do not take off the seatbelt for any reason unless I tell you it is okay. If I get into trouble, you just push the microphone button and tell dispatch that I am in trouble, then sit and wait for other cops to arrive."

Some of the male cops would let Lissa answer the radio calls, others let her keep the activity log or complete offense reports. Lissa knew that this was the career path that she wanted to take.

In her second year of the program, Lissa got the chance to actually answer 9-1-1 calls and dispatch the cops because of a female communication supervisor who saw potential in this young girl. In her senior year of high school Lissa was promoted to Lieutenant of the Explorer Post, second in command.

Lissa was riding with Toni on a weekend evening shift when a Chevrolet came screaming around a corner almost hitting a parked car. Toni ordered Lissa to activate the overhead lights and the car pulled over almost immediately. Lissa sat in the car and watched as Toni neared the driver's side window. Lissa then heard two shots and watched in horror as Toni dropped to the ground. As she had been instructed, Lissa screamed into the radio that an officer was down on Main Street just north of Broad. Unlike what she had been instructed, Lissa jumped out of the car and ran up to the down officer.

Grabbing the officer's gun from her holster, Lissa fired at the vehicle until the slide of the semi-automatic pistol locked open.

Lissa had fired sixteen shots. She knew that she had blown out the rear window of the vehicle with at least one of the shots.

Focusing her attention on Toni, Lissa ripped open her uniform shirt and looked in amazement to the two bullets that were imbedded in Toni's bulletproof vest. Toni was moaning in pain as police cars arrived from all directions. Lissa laid the gun down on the ground and saw that she was bleeding from the recoil of the slide of the gun firing. When the paramedic unit arrived at the scene, there was a question as to whether they could treat Lissa without her parents' consent since she was a juvenile. Lissa became an instant legend with the cops who nicknamed her the "terror of Lafollette".

After the paramedics did only what was necessary to stop the bleeding, a male cop drove her to her house and told her parents to take her to the emergency room to be checked out.

The story was on the front page of the local newspaper and on television the next day. The suspects in the shooting were captured by the Kentucky State Police driving northbound on I-75. Lissa had indeed shot out the rear window of the car and hit the passenger in the shoulder with another round.

***

As graduation from high school got closer, her parents sat her down to talk about her future. Her dad told her, "We put away money for both you and your brother to attend college, but your brother decided he had all the education he wanted and decided he enjoyed fixing cars. That means that the money saved is all yours to pay for school. Do you know where you want to attend college and what you want to major in?" Lissa had already done her homework. She told her parents, "Eastern Kentucky University has one of the most acclaimed criminal justice programs in the US and it is less than one hundred miles from home." Her mom said, "Money will still be very tight, so you will have to find a job there if you want spending money." Lissa smiled and said, "That sounds like fun."

Lissa knew that she had breezed through high school and saw no issues with college life. At five feet eight inches tall and weighing one hundred twenty-five pounds, she had always been athletic, playing varsity basketball, volleyball, and softball for her school. She had actually hoped to get an athletic scholarship, but that just never materialized.

When she arrived at the Dispatch Center for her shift, she told the supervisor where she would be attending college and that she was told by her parents that she needed to find a job. The supervisor said that she would contact the Richmond, Kentucky Public Safety Communications Center and put in a good word for her. The supervisor, who had over twenty years of service with the City started to give serious instruction, teaching Lissa how to access the

National Crime Information Center (NCIC), the Tennessee Bureau of Investigation database, and how to access criminal records through the multi-state III system.

Just prior to leaving for the campus, Lissa stopped by the Communication Center to thank the woman for all her teaching. The supervisor told Lisa, "When you are settled in
Richmond, call the Public Safety Center and ask for Denise Thomas. She has a part-time job for you there."

Lissa's parents drove her north to the campus and helped her load her stuff into the dorm room. They told her that they could not afford to buy a car for her. The room was broken into two sections, each with a desk and a bed. Her new roommate was already in the room and was putting her clothing in her side of the room.

Lissa introduced herself to the pretty young black woman who told Lissa that her name was Diana Rose and that she was from Lexington, Kentucky. Diana said, "I am here to get my degree in nursing so I can be a psych nurse. What are you going for?" Lissa replied, "Criminal Justice."

The first few days were pure chaos as Lissa was attempting to find her classes and get adjusted to college life. She liked the fact that her roommate was as passionate about nursing as Lissa was about becoming a cop.

Once she had settled into her new life, Lissa made the call to the Richmond Public Safety Communications Center and scheduled an interview with Denise Thomas. She arrived for the meeting and found Ms. Thomas to be about fifty years old with a smile that could illuminate the City. Thomas told Lissa that based upon the recommendation given by the supervisor from Tennessee, she was prepared to make a job offer if Lissa passed the background check and polygraph examination. Thomas told Lissa, "Because of your age, the background check is a formality, but is there anything that is going to come up in the lie detector that is going to create a problem?" Lissa smiled and said simply, "No ma'am.

The lie detector test was administered by the Kentucky
State Police in a room at the Richland Police Department. The examiner was a twenty-four year veteran of KSP and had been doing polygraph tests for the past eleven years.
He could immediately tell that the young girl was

extremely nervous, so he asked, "Have you ever taken a lie detector test before?" Lissa meekly replied, "No, sir." The examiner asked a set of standardized questions prepared by the City of Richmond, making sure that there no ambiguous questions. When the interview portion was complete, he wired Lissa up to the machine, being very careful to keep her as relaxed as possible. When he turned the machine on, he laughed and told Lissa, "You really are nervous. Your heartbeat is up to ninety-eight beats per minute." Seeing the alarm in the young girl's face, the examiner said, "It's okay, the machine actually understands that you are nervous. She was actually only wired up to the machine for about ten minutes, but it felt like a lifetime to her. As the examiner took the wires off her, he said, "I wish you well in your new position, because I found nothing that would exclude you." Lissa thanked the man profusely and left the police station to go back to her dorm. It only took two days for Lissa to receive a call with a job offer. She would work first shift on Saturdays and Sundays through the school session and be able to work full-time during the summer. She was looking forward to getting started in a paid position. ***

The first year went quickly for Lissa. She and Diana were good friends and would socialize in their free time. They found their career choices offered them common ground to exchange ideas and to have differing views on the same topic. The only time that Lissa was able to get home was over the Christmas break and she had to take a Greyhound Bus to get there. Her parents drove her back to the school so she did not have to lose any work.

The second year classes brought much more of a challenge as Lissa signed up for forensic science and cyber crime courses. The forensic training made her laugh at the things that were done on television programs and in computer crime she learned how to hack computers and how to break passwords.

Her dispatching job was a learning experience as well. The first pursuit she handled brought back memories of Toni being shot. Since she also handled fire dispatches, she took a lot of calls around the campus for out-of-control frat parties and stupid injuries suffered by the students. Mostly it was the same as in Lafollette, a small town with not a lot of crime. Diana met a guy and decided to drop out of school to get married.

***

Lissa breezed through the last two years and felt like she was ready to join the workforce. As her graduation was approaching, Denise from the Public Safety Center offered her a full-time position. Lisa told the supervisor that she would only be interested in full-time employment with the Police Department, but that offer never came.

Lissa's mom, dad, and brother arrived for the graduation ceremony in two different cars. When Lissa questioned why they didn't ride together, her dad kissed her on the cheek and said, "The Ford Escape is for you to start your new life. Where do you intend to go to find a job?" Lissa thought for a moment and replied, "I was thinking Cincinnati because they have a well-respected police department.

CHAPTER TWO

Lissa drove north up I-71 until it merged with I-75 just south of Cincinnati. She saw a billboard for a motel with weekly rates in Florence, Kentucky, just eight miles from the Ohio line. Lissa checked into the motel and paid for one week with cash. Her room was meager with just a bed, dresser, a small television, small refrigerator, and a microwave. Using her savings from her job, Lissa figured she would be able to survive about six months. She would use her time to find employment.

Her parents had bought her a laptop computer to help with her studies and the motel had a wifi hookup so she could job and apartment hunt online. It only took two days for her to find an apartment she liked. It was in Newport, Kentucky, just a bridge from Cincinnati. An elderly woman owned the house. Because it was too large for her, she transformed it into a duplex making the rear the entrance to the apartment. The old lady liked this young woman and offered her a rate much less than the motel was charging and it was a one bedroom that was already furnished. Although the furniture was dated, it offered a comfortable place from which to get started. All Lissa had to do was buy a television, get cable and internet service and she was ready for the next step. Lissa found a job opportunity online at the corporate headquarters of a national retail outlet in downtown Cincinnati. She filled out the online application and moved on to looking for police employment in the area.

The next day she received a telephone call from the Human Resources Department of the retailer. The woman asked the standard questions that employers ask, one of which was, "Where do you expect to be in five years?" Lissa did not hesitate when she replied, "I expect to be a Cincinnati Police Officer by then." Thinking that her answer blew any chance of getting that job, Lissa began looking at other opportunities. She was surprised when she opened her email to find a time and date for her interview with the manager of the security department.

Lissa arrived for the interview wearing a pantsuit that contoured tightly to her five-foot eight inch frame. She approached one of the two desk guards and told him she was there for an interview. The guard made a call and told her the Security Manager would be right with her.

The Security Manager came out into the lobby and introduced himself as Denis Wilson. He led her into a cluttered office with a wall of video cameras and two desks. Wilson told her that he too was a graduate of EKU criminal Justice and they chatted about the professors that they shared. He asked, "Did you really tell the HR woman that you intend to be a Cincinnati cop within the next five years?" Lissa replied, "That is my goal." He told her that the job was not police work and that it would be a second shift position that only paid twelve dollars per hour. Lissa said she had no problem with that. She said, "I need a job to get established in the Cincinnati area and I will perform the job to the best of my ability." Wilson told her that she would be receiving an e-mail job offer after the background check, which would take two to three weeks.

Exactly two weeks later Lissa opened her e-mail to find a job offer confirmation and a starting date for the position of Security Officer. She was told to report for orientation the following Monday morning at eight o'clock in the morning. After the two-hour orientation, she was assigned to a Security Supervisor who gave her a tour of the facility and an overview of the job. She spent the first week watching and performing the tasks of checking in visitors and contractors at the lobby console, performing security checks of the floors and operating the extensive camera system.

At the beginning of the second week, Lissa was provided her schedule of second shift working with a partner. Her regular partner was a twenty-four year old male named William Workman, who told Lissa that he was currently in the process to join the Cincinnati Police Department.
Lissa was being flirted with by almost all of the junior executives as they were leaving work. Her five foot eight inch one hundred twenty-pound frame fit well into the black shirt and grey pant uniform of the Security Department. She loved the attention that she was getting from the male employees, who made her blush with their complimentary comments. Lissa started talking with a twenty-nine year old man who worked in the Legal Department and finally agreed to meet him for lunch

before work. It would be her first 'date' since arriving in Cincinnati. The lunch went really well and she liked talking to this man. She agreed to join him for a drink after her shift. They met at a little hole-in-the-wall called the Knock Back directly across the street from the corporate office. They listened to the live music chatting amicably until he put his hand on her inner thigh. She quickly removed it and told the man in no uncertain terms, "I am a virgin and intend to stay that way until I am married." She thanked him for the drinks and walked back to her car in the parking lot and drove home.

CHAPTER THREE

It was just another Tuesday when Lissa arrived for her shift. From three until seven, both her and Bill remained busy checking people out for the day. Bill took the first building round while Lissa manned the lobby console. At nine p.m., it was Lissa's turn to make her rounds. She started on the twenty-first floor and worked her way down, floor by floor checking to make sure that nothing was out of the ordinary.

She was walking on the eighth floor when she suddenly felt a sharp pain on the left side of her face that knocked her to the floor. Then she felt a man's hand unbuckling her belt and pulling her pants down to ankles, her bare ass exposed. She screamed out, but there was no one else on the floor to hear her. When the man entered her vagina breaking the hymen, Lissa cried out in pain. She felt the pulsing of man ejaculating inside of her and tears of pain and frustration were pouring down her face. When he was done raping her, the man got up and walked toward an exit door that led onto a patio and then into a parking garage.

Bill began to worry when he had not heard from Lissa in over twenty minutes. He called out on the portable twoway radio, but received no response. The last time he had heard from her she was on the eighth floor, so Bill secured the entrances and rode the elevator up to the floor to attempt to locate her. When the elevator door opened, Bill heard a whimpering sound coming from the hallway. Bill ran down the hallway and saw

Lissa laying on the floor with her pants down around her ankles softly crying. Using his personal cellphone, Bill called 9-1-1 requesting police assistance. Bill did not want to leave his partner alone, but the police would not be able to enter. Ripping off his jacket, he gently laid it on Lissa's bare ass and told her he would be back with the police. Bill met two Cincinnati Police officers at the lobby door and took them to the eighth floor where Lissa had not moved. One of the officers called for a paramedic unit and the other asked Lissa what had happened. All Lissa could tell the officers was that she had been sucker punched and then raped by a male who was wearing a mask over his face. The cops told Bill to go back to the lobby and wait for the paramedic unit to arrive. When Bill arrived in the lobby, the paramedics were standing at the entrance. He told the medics that his partner had been assaulted and raped, so they went back to their unit to get a gurney to transport the victim to the hospital.

Bill called the Security Manager to advise him what had occurred and then returned to the eighth floor where the medics were tending to Lissa. They carefully placed a sheet on her before removing Bill's jacket. The cops told Bill that his jacket might contain trace evidence and would be kept by police. The medics used a backboard so that Lissa, who was still crying softly, could be rolled over without exposing her nakedness any more that necessary. Lissa was transported to the University of Cincinnati Medical Center by the medics.

****

Lissa was taken into a private area of the Emergency Room where she was met by a nurse who introduced herself as Carole and said, "I am a Sexual Assault Nurse Examiner and have received special training in the collection of evidence. I cannot tell you that I understand what you are experiencing, but I can tell you that I want to make sure that any evidence is properly collected so the sonofabitch who did this spends a long time in the Ohio Penal System. I will treat you with the utmost respect and dignity." Lissa tried to smile, but the pain and humiliation were clearly apparent on her face. The nurse completed the rape kit quickly and the doctor came in and administered a sedative so that Lissa could sleep.

When Lissa woke in a hospital room, she immediately focused on a man and woman standing at the far side of the room. The woman, who was wearing a pantsuit, opened her jacket to show a badge hanging on her belt. She told Lissa, "My name is Detective Robin Miller and this is my partner Detective Willie Brown. If you would like to only talk with a woman, my partner will leave and wait for us to finish." Lissa just nodded her head and Det. Brown immediately left the room.

Miller said, "I am not going to tell you that I know what you are experiencing, but I have been investigating sexual assault cases for the past ten years and I want you to know that you will be treated with respect. I will tell you what we know so far, and then I need to get your statement of whatever you remember. I understand that you went to college for this, so I need you to use that knowledge to help us catch this motherfucker. We know that the suspect entered the building through the patio entrance on the eighth floor by forcing a lock on one of the glass doors. The camera caught him entering and leaving, but he was wearing a mask and a hoodie, so we do not have a face shot of him. Do you mind if I record your statement so that we get everything correct?"

Lissa nodded in the affirmative and Det. Miller pulled out a small recording device and set it on the bed. Lissa spoke softly as she said, "I was walking down the hallway when I felt a sharp pain on the left side of my face. When I hit the floor, I saw a male standing over me. He bent down and I felt him unbuckling my belt and then felt my pants being pulled down to my ankles. I screamed out, but there was no one to hear me. I heard him unzipping his pants and then felt him spreading my legs. I screamed in pain when he inserted his penis into my vagina and I felt the pulsing of him ejaculating into me. He got up and zipped up his pants and I saw him turn and walk away. I never did get a good look at him. The hoodie was grey and the mask over his face was black. He did not speak the entire time."

Det. Miller said, "I want you to call me Robin and that was great. Do you think he was wearing a condom?" "No, Robin, I don't because I felt a hot sensation going up inside me." Robin said softly, "That means we will be able to get a DNA sample and, hopefully, we will have his DNA or it will be in C.O.D.I.S." Do you know what CODIS is?" Lissa answered simply, "Yes, I learned about it at Eastern Kentucky University. It is the national database for DNA coordinated by the FBI." Robin said, "I would really like to get a picture of the left side of your face in the hope we can get an imprint of his knuckles. Do you mind if my partner comes in and takes a few pictures? None of them will be of your private parts."

Det. Miller called in her partner and he got close-up shots of the marks on Lissa's left cheek. Robin told Lissa, "We are going to let you alone to collect your thoughts. If you need ANYTHING, call this number twenty-four hours a day and I will call you back within minutes, okay? Is there anyone you want me call and tell what happened to you?" Lissa said "no" and tried to smile, but the painkillers were kicking in and she went back to sleep.

When she woke, the nurse told her she was being released from the hospital and a man, who was claiming to be her partner, was waiting to take her home. Lisa asked, "Is his name Bill?" The nurse said "yes" and helped Lisa get ready to go home. She was only wearing a hospital gown because the police had taken all her clothing as evidence. When they got into Bill's car, Lissa told him she wanted to get her car back and drive home herself. Bill told her, "Everyone at work is sick over what happened to you. They all said if you need anything, just call and we will come running." Lissa felt the honesty in his voice, but wanted to be alone until the soreness went away.

Lissa was not home an hour when she got a phone call from the Security Manager telling her to take as long as she needed to recover. He said, "The Company will pay your salary for as long as you are off."

***

Lissa laid around her apartment watching television and taking pain meds for the next two days. She was watching TV when the phone rang. The call was from Det. Miller who said, "Lissa, this is Robin. The Police Department has a strict policy of not identifying victims of sexual assault, but I saw a strength in you that, if you are willing to go public, would help other victims. Would you be willing to be interviewed by a friend of mine who is married to a retired Lieutenant from this department?" Lissa thought for a moment and replied, "Let me think about it and I will get back to you." Robin continued, "It appears that it will take four to six weeks to get the results of the DNA evidence back from the lab, but we are focusing all of our attention on getting this bastard." Lissa said, "I don't need to think about it. If you trust the reporter, I will do an interview." Robin screamed, "Great, I will have her call you today."

Within the hour Lissa received a call from Deb Fixen of WKRC-TV News. They set a time for her to come over with her videographer and hung up the phone. Lissa was extremely nervous when she opened the door, but the smile on the reporter's face was comforting and soothing. Fixen said,

"Robin told me you are a strong woman and this can help a lot of victims. I will put nothing on the air that will tell where you live or make you look bad in any way. On that you can depend!" The interview lasted almost an hour. Without getting into the specifics of the act of rape, Lissa talked about her emotions and the pain she was suffering. At the end of the interview, Fixen told Lissa that the airing would be "explosive".

The interview led the six o'clock news and ran almost three minutes, which is an extraordinary amount of time for a single story. Det. Miller talked about the investigation and the strength of character of the victim.

The story showed the entrance to the corporate headquarters where the rape took place and talked about the lack of training and equipment that the security officers were given to perform their jobs. To say the least, the corporate retailer was taking a public relations beating.

The Facebook page at WKRC ran wild with comments from the viewers about the story. People were threatening to boycott the retailer, there were threats of violent retaliation against the retailer for failing to protect this young woman, and offers to personally castrate the perpetrator of this act of violence. The story was picked up by the Associated Press newswire and the network news and the outpouring of support for Lissa and outrage for the retailer and the suspect was palpable.

Robin called after the story aired and told Lissa, "I just got off the phone with an attorney friend of mine. This guy represented a cop who was in deep shit and got him out of it. He says you have a clear civil case against the employer for failing to adequately provide for your safety and he is willing to represent you for free. It is totally up to you. At least take a moment and talk to him. His name is Timothy Cusher." Lissa decided to take a break and make a decision on that at a later time.

The next afternoon Lissa got a call from a man claiming to be an attorney for her employer. He asked Lissa how she was doing and if the company could do anything to help her recovery. He said the company would pay for any medical or psychological services that Lissa felt she needed and that her job was secure for the foreseeable future. He gave her his direct line and told him to call her for anything she needed.

No sooner than she hung up the phone, it rang again. A male voice said, "Melissa, my name is Robert Goins and I am the Chief of Investigations for the Kentucky Attorney General. The AG would like to meet with you personally, but before we talk about the specifics, I need you to do something for me. I want you to call me back on our 800 number. You can get it in the phone book, and, when they answer, ask for me. That will verify that this call is authentic."

Lissa went online and found the toll free number and called it. The receptionist transferred the call immediately and the male answered, "Robert Goins, hello Melissa. Are you satisfied that this call is real?" Lissa answered in a quizzical voice, "yes, sir." Goins said, "The AG's Office was in the process of establishing a sexual assault crimes task force and the AG would like to come to Northern Kentucky to talk to you about becoming an investigator for the Unit. The AG will meet you at the Florence Police Department if that is okay with you."

The meeting was scheduled for three days later and she arrived at the PD just as a black Cadillac pulled up. Two men in suits jumped out of the car and opened the back door for a man in his forties. They looked like bodyguards to Lissa. She followed the three into the front entrance where one of the bodyguards told the receptionist that they were expected and had a conference room reserved.

The bodyguard said they were expecting a woman named Melissa Harding and that she was to be immediately brought to the conference room. Lissa softly said, "That would be me" surprising the three men. The receptionist escorted the four back to a large conference room and the two bodyguards positioned themselves on the outside of the door as their boss and Lissa went in.

The AG started the conversation with, "Melissa, we have been discussing forming a task force to help local police with sexual assault investigations. I saw the story that was done on you and we did our own background investigation of you before making you an offer to become the Unit's first investigator. The position would be based in Kenton County so that you do not have to relocate. You will be provided a state vehicle, and we will find you an office and send you back to Eastern Kentucky to become a certified state investigator. Are you interested?" Without waiting for an answer, he continued, "You will bring a perspective that few can offer. You can actually tell the victims that you understand the feelings of terror and humiliation and that will make them more comfortable about talking about the specifics of their traumatic incident. The starting salary would be fifty-two thousand dollars per year with state benefits and pension. We will send you anywhere in the Commonwealth that requests the assistance of the Unit. You will have the opportunity to actually impact the victims and put the perpetrators in the penitentiary. You will report directly to my Chief of Investigations, but you will also have a direct pipeline to me. Please don't say no."

Lissa smiled and said, "My friends call me Lissa and I would love to call you Boss!" The AG ended the interview with, "There is a certification program starting in eight weeks and we will enroll you in it if that is not too soon. We will get you your car and office space in the next few days." Lissa thanked the man and watched him drive away in total amazement.

CHAPTER FOUR

Then Lissa arrived home from the whirlwind meeting with the Attorney General, the message light on her phone was flashing wildly. She played the message which said, "This is the attorney from the Corporate Office. We spoke on the phone earlier. Please call me as soon as you receive this." Lisa dialed the number and the man said, "We have talked extensively about your situation and understand that you might not want to return to our employment based upon the traumatic experience that you endured. Should you decide not to return, we are prepared to offer you a severance package of two hundred thousand dollars. All we ask in return is a signed release of liability from you."

Lissa said simply, "I will give you an answer in the next few days." Lisa hung up with the attorney and looked for the phone number of the attorney recommended by Robin. She called Cusher and told him about the call from the attorney. There was a long pause of silence and then Cusher said, "Melissa, you can probably get a lot more than that should you decide to sue, but it is possible you could get less. There is also the consideration of being all over the news and whether or not that might impact your future employment decisions." Lissa said, "I didn't tell him that I just accepted a job as an investigator for the Kentucky Attorney General." Cusher appeared to be laughing uncontrollably and it took a minute for him to get his breath. He said, "Take their offer and spend it wisely. You have no need for my services. God's speed young lady. When they provide you with the release, tell them to send it to me and then you will sign it." Lissa called the attorney back and told him that she would accept his offer and to mail the release to Timothy Cusher, Attorney at Law, for her signature. When the release arrived at Cusher's office, he called the attorney and asked why the check was not attached?" The check was sent by courier and Lissa went to Cusher's office and she signed it. Lissa was waiting to hear from the AG's office and beginning to get nervous because it been almost two weeks.

Her phone rang and the caller identified himself as a trooper with the Kentucky State Police. He said he was calling because her car was waiting at a Ford dealership in Erlanger, Kentucky and he was to come pick her up to get it. When the two arrived at the dealership, the salesman handed her a set of keys and pointed to a royal blue Ford Crown Victoria parked in the front of the building. Lissa got in and checked the odometer which had just over six miles on it.

The trooper opened the driver's door and told Lissa to push the toggle switch next to the radio on the dashboard. He motioned her to get out of the car and they walked to the front where Lissa saw red and blue lights flashing in every direction. There was a red and a blue strobe in the front grill, the turn signal lights were flashing red and blue and there was a light bar flashing from the top of the windshield. When the two got to the rear of the car, there were strobes flashing brightly from both sides of the rear deck. The trooper laughed and said, "No one will be able to say they didn't see you coming!" The trooper told Lissa that they needed to go to the State Police Post in Dry Ridge, Kentucky for the rest of her equipment. He said that her new badge and identification card would be there for her. The County Judge Executive administered her oath of office and the State Police took her picture for her photo identification card and showed her the hi-tech communication system which would allow her to talk to every large police agency in the Commonwealth.

***

Melissa arrived at the Kentucky training facility twenty minutes before her scheduled starting time and the receptionist manning the desk appeared none too happy. She told Lissa that she would be unable to get her room until after her training day and that she was to immediately report to the firearm training facility on the other side of the campus. The receptionist gave Lissa a map showing all of the police training centers throughout the Richmond campus.

Lissa walked into the firearm training center and was surprised to see she was the only one there. A man, who appeared to be in his mid-sixties. walked up to her and said, "Hello, my name is John Bushum and I am a firearm training instructor for the Commonwealth of Kentucky.

You must be Melissa Harding." Melissa smiled and said simply, "Yes, sir.", Bushum continued, "I have been teaching firearms for well over thirty years, so you will leave here comfortable

27

with the weapons you will have access to for your job. Have you ever actually fired a weapon before?" Lissa said, "While a police explorer in Tennessee, I emptied my trainer's 40 caliber handgun into a car after they shot the officer." Bushum appeared astonished as he said, "You mean there really is a 'terror of Lafollette'? We all thought that story was a fable." Lissa said, "The only problem was that I cut my hand into shreds firing the gun!" Bushum laughed and said, "Two things, first your hands have grown since then and second, I will get you a grip that works."

Bushum handed her a box with a 40 caliber Sig Sauer handgun and a black leather holster and said, "This will be your assigned weapon. We will spend the next three days teaching you to load, unload, draw, fire, and fix malfunctions on this gun. We will spend day four with the Remington 870 shotgun and day five will be shooting the tactical rifle. Let's get to work!"

Bushum appeared impressed at how quickly Lissa learned to be an accomplished shooter and the three days passed very quickly. The only issue came when Lissa had to look down to draw her weapon or re-holster it. Every time she would look down, Bushum would slap the back of her hand. She finally looked at the instructor and said, "That REALLY hurts!" Bushum did not bat an eye as he looked at her and said, "It hurts a helluva lot less than being put in a box and then dropped into a hole in the ground. You NEVER take your eyes of the threat in front of you!"

When they got to the shotgun, Bushum demonstrated the proper stance, grip and firing procedure. He handed the shotgun to Lissa and told her to load one round into the weapon and then fire it. When the butt of the shotgun slammed into her shoulder from the recoil, Lissa let out a scream. Bushum smiled and said, "That is going to leave a mark! Next time you will actually pay attention." Day five was the AR-15 tactical rifle which had a switch offering three firing options. The first was firing a single shot every time the trigger was pulled, the second fired three bullets each time the trigger was depressed, and the last option was fully automatic.

At the end of the day Bushum smiled and said, "Remind me never to piss you off. You will do fine. Have a great career."

***

Week two would be self-defense. Lissa was melded in with a police recruit class so that she would have a partner to practice with. She was paired with a Hopkinsville Police Officer who was a defensive lineman. The instructor told Lissa to place the big man under arrest and get him handcuffed. When she grabbed his arm, he picked her up off the ground and laughed. The instructor, also a female, walked over to the student and said, "Now, do that to me!" She grabbed his arm and he went to pick her up just like he had with the other girl. He found himself laying on the padded mat feeling a sharp pain in his left leg from where the instructor had kicked his leg out from under him. Now the rest of the class was laughing.

They were well into the second day of class when Lissa began feeling dizzy and weak. The instructor decided she could not continue until she was cleared by the college medical center. Another instructor took her to the clinic where a nurse checked her vital signs and took blood to test. After about a thirty minute wait, a doctor came into the room and said, "Are you aware that you are pregnant?" The shocked look on Lissa's face answered the question. She said in a shaky voice, "Are you sure?" The doctor said he was positive and they had even run the test twice to confirm.

Lissa went back to her room and sobbed uncontrollably. She had some decisions to make and felt totally alone. Her religion taught abortion was wrong and she was not in a position to be a single mother at this point in her life. She cussed the bastard who did this to her and vowed to make him pay.

The doctor cleared her to continue her training, but she thought of the man who had raped her every time she had a male partner and the poor guy paid dearly for having the misfortune of being paired with her.

CHAPTER FIVE

Melisa moved into her new office which was set up for her in the Commonwealth Attorney's Office in the Kenton County building in Covington, Kentucky.

When she entered the main doors on the first day, she was greeted by a woman in her early fifties seated at the reception desk. Melissa flashed her gold star badge emboldened with "Investigator, Commonwealth of Kentucky, Office of the Attorney General" on it. The receptionist smiled and said, "Hi, I am Mindy, your office is this way." The office looked like it was intended for an attorney. It had a big mahogany desk, a computer, telephone, copier, bookshelves, and a fax machine.

As she sat at the big desk she could not help but focus on her pregnancy and what she was going to do. She was staring at the blank computer screen when her personal cell phone rang. When she answered the caller said, "Hi, Lissa. This is Robin from Cincinnati Police. We got a C.O.D.I.S. hit on the DNA and I was wondering if you could come to the Criminal Investigation Section to take a look at a photo lineup. Maybe we could have lunch after?" Lissa said, "I can be there in about twenty minutes" and then hung up. Lissa parked her unmarked car in front of the CIS building in a spot for police vehicles only. She placed a placard on the dashboard that said. "POLICE Commonwealth of Kentucky" on it. She rode the elevator up to the fifth floor and, without thinking, walked through the metal detector at the entrance setting off the alarm. Two detectives, with their guns drawn, came running out of the back of the office until they heard a woman scream, "STAND DOWN, she is here to see me"? Lissa sheepishly opened her jacket to show the cops her badge and they returned to whatever it was that they were doing.

Lissa told Robin about her new job and the two got a laugh out of scaring the male superheroes. Robin laid down a sheet of paper in front of Lissa with six pictures of similar looking males and asked if she could identify any of the men. Lissa looked at the pictures and said, "Robin, I told you I never did get a look at the man's face." Robin replied, "I had to try. We have signed warrants on the suspect who's DNA we retrieved and are trying to locate him now. If I give you any more information at this point, it could taint our criminal case, so you will just have to trust me on this. Now let's go get lunch"

They rode to a restaurant in Lissa's new car and Robin seemed really impressed with Lissa's new job. It was at lunch that Lissa told Robin about being pregnant by the bastard and that, due to religious beliefs, abortion was out of the question. As Lissa went to drop Robin off at the office, Robin said, "As soon as we are able to locate him, I will call you. I promised to keep you in the loop throughout."

   ***

Lissa was at home in bed, still tossing and turning from the stress, when her work cell rang. The caller said, "This is Kentucky State Police Dispatch. You have been requested by Augusta, Kentucky Police to assist them in a rape that just occurred. They want you to meet them at the hospital in Augusta."

Lissa jumped out of bed and quickly dressed for the ride. Augusta is approximately sixty miles east of Cincinnati on the river. She set the car's GPS and followed the direction with her blue lights and siren on the whole trip. She arrived at the hospital and met a detective in the emergency room. The detective introduced himself as Bill O'Donnel and said, "The victim is a forty-year-old white woman who was found walking down a road naked from the waist down. She has refused to talk to any of us and we hoped that she might talk to you."

Lissa walked into the treatment room where the crying woman was laying on the bed. She opened her jacket so the woman could see her badge and said, "My name is Melissa Harding and I am an investigator for the Kentucky Attorney General's Office Sexual Assault Task Force. I actually do understand what you are going through. I understand the feelings of embarrassment, humiliation, frustration, and anger because I was the victim of a rape on my last job. The bastard stole my virginity and now I am pregnant with his child. That is why I took this job, to help others. Are you willing to tell me what happened? By the way, my friends call me Lissa, so why don't you call me that, too. Let's start with your name."

"My name is Vivian Principle and I am willing to tell you what happened because I believe you really care" the woman said. "I went to the Knotty Pine Bar to have a few drinks. I drove there in my car, but felt woozy when I was ready to leave and only live a half mile away. I was walking home when a car pulled up next to me and the passenger window rolled down.

The man driving pointed a gun at me and told me to get into the car or he would kill me. He drove down the road and turned down a dirt road just outside of town. He ordered me to take off my pants and get into the back seat on my hands and knees. I was crying and he told me to shut up and not make a sound or he would kill me right there. He spread the cheeks of my ass with his hands and then and forced himself into my ass. It hurt like hell but I was afraid to scream because of his threats. As soon as he shot his load he pulled his penis out and grabbed me by the hair, pulling me out of the back seat. He pushed me to the ground and then walked around to the driver's side of the car and drove off, leaving me there with no pants.

I was walking toward the main road when a couple drove up on me and brought me here."

Lissa told the woman, "I want to take this one step at a time so that we get the sonofabitch and put him where he will never hurt another woman. I am going to get a specially trained nurse to come in and complete a rape kit. She will have been certified as a Sexual Assault Nurse Examiner. Is that okay with you?" Vivian sobbed softly and nodded her head. Lissa went to the ER room desk and had them contact their S.A.N.E nurse on call.

Walking out to where O"Donnel had been cooling his heels for the last forty-five minutes, Lissa tried to bring him up to speed, telling him, "The victim has told me what happened, but there is much more information I am going to need to develop. I am waiting on the rape kit and then I will get more answers. You can either wait or return to the PD and I will come there when I get done because she is not likely to want to talk with you present." O'Donnel nodded that he understood and told Lissa he would meet her at the station.

When the nurse had completed her work, Lissa returned to the room. She pulled a chair up next to the bed and looked Vivian in the eye as she asked, "Let's talk about the car first. What can you tell me about it?" Vivian thought for a second and said, "The car was white and it had big round headlights, like a vintage car. The interior was red and the seats were leather. I did not see a license plate to get a number and there was no light on the plate." Lissa next asked, "Tell me about the man. Had you ever seen him before?" Vivian replied that she did not know him. Lissa asked, "Describe him for me?" Vivian said, "He was a white guy, over six feet and on the heavy side. He was wearing a brown flannel shirt and blue jeans and had a mustache and looked like he had no shaved in several days." Lissa said, "I need to ask this. Do you believe he was wearing a condom?" Vivian sobbed and said, "No, definitely not. I felt a hot sensation over the pain when he shot his load and I felt something leaking out of my butt as I walked down the road."

Just then a doctor walked into the room and told Vivian that he needed to check her anus for any possible damage that may have resulted from the penetration. Lissa told Victoria that she was going to leave, but would be back in touch later in the day, after Victoria had some time to rest.

Lissa drove to the PD and filled O'Donnel in on what she knew. O'Donnel told her that the Police Chief had gotten Lissa a reservation at a nearby hotel and that they could resume after Lissa had gotten a few hours of sleep. He would meet her at the PD at three o'clock that afternoon. It was almost six a.m. when Lissa collapsed on the bed in the hotel.

Lissa and Det. O'Donnel drove to the Knotty Pine Bar to see if they had any cameras. The bar had a surveillance camera covering the parking lot and the two cops got a copy to take back and watch. They decided that they needed to return to the bar in the late evening hours to see if the car was there, or if anyone saw anything. They decided to meet at ten p.m. and that O'Donnel would check the parking lot for the car on the camera.

When Lissa arrived at ten o'clock, O'Donnel was smiling. He said, "I found a vintage Ford Fairlane with round headlights on the cam." He showed Lissa the still picture of the car that he had printed. When they walked into the bar at ten thirty, there were only six customers to be seen and all were male. The men started catcalling and commenting on Lissa's looks. Lissa could see that O'Donnel was getting ready to say or do something, so she nudged him and signaled him to remain cool.

A large frame man got out of his chair and said, "Hey honey, come over and join a real man!" Lissa pulled O'Donnel back signaling him to wait and walked over to the man. When she got close enough, she placed her hand softly on the man's thigh and almost immediately locked in a vice grip on the man's testicles. She looked up into his bulging eyes and said, "You are going to help me find the man who raped a woman who was here last night. Do you understand?" The man, who was standing on his tiptoes softly replied, "Yes, ma'am. I do." The other five men stood up intending to help their friend in distress until they saw O'Donnel draw his service weapon and drop it to his side. Deciding the guy was not a friend worth dying for, the men all sat back down.

Without loosening her grip on the big guy's balls, Lissa produced the picture of the car and said, "You are going to tell me who owns this car and where we can find him, understand?" The man told the two cops that the owner of the car was Charlie Sheen, no relation to the actor, and that he lived in the Meadows Trailer Park two miles down the road on the left. Lissa looked at the guy and said, "I am going to let go now. If you move, my partner is going to put a bullet between your eyes! Oh, and thank you for your cooperation." The two cops backed out of the bar and went back to O'Donnel's unmarked unit.

They drove down to the trailer park entrance and found the manager's trailer. The manager told them that Sheen lived in last trailer on the right, but he had left over an hour ago in his car. O'Donnel showed the manager the picture of the car and the manager said that it was Sheen's car. O'Donnel called for a team to stake out the trailer and the two drove to the hospital so Lissa could give the victim an update.

When Lissa walked into the hospital room, she could see that Victoria was in serious pain. Vivian cried as she said the man who raped her caused tearing in the anal cavity and that it would require surgery. She lit up when Lissa told her that they had a suspect and were trying to locate him now. The small smile that Lissa saw on the woman's face made the lack of sleep worthwhile.

When Lissa got back to the car where O'Donnel was waiting, he told her, "Detectives canvased the neighbors and learned that our suspect told them he was heading to visit friends in West Virginia and would be back in a couple of weeks. You can head home and we will call you when we snatch him up." On the drive home, Lissa felt good about what she had accomplished. She knew that all of the cases would not be this easy to solve, but that she was in the right job for her.

***

Once back in her office, Lissa created her first case file and made a copy for her supervisor. She sent a copy of the complete file to Frankfort for her supervisor and waited to hear back from Augusta PD for the apprehension.

She was sitting in her office when the phone rang. It was Robin telling her that Cincinnati had found the location of her rapist and he was in Kentucky. Lissa wrote down all of the information about the location and went off to find a Judge to get a search warrant. She found the Kenton County Commonwealth Attorney sitting in his office and he called a judge friend to sign the warrant. Robin and her partner met Lissa at her office and they went to the Judge with an affidavit already prepared by Robin and the warrant was signed. The suspect was believed to be in a residence in Elsmere, Kentucky, just a little over six miles from Lissa's office. Lissa contacted the Elsmere Police who only had one car on duty and then the Kenton County Police for backup.

The State Police had provided her with a bulletproof vest with the word "POLICE" imprinted on the front and back. The uniform officers covered the front and back entrance while

Robin, her male partner, and Lissa kicked in the front door. They went three different directions in search of the suspect, a twenty-nine year old with a history of sexual assaults. Lissa entered a bedroom and found the suspect hiding behind a door. The man, Paul Guildis, had a knife in his hand while Lissa was holding her AR-15 rifle. Lissa said, "Please come at me with that knife you spineless cocksucker and let me splatter your guts all over this room!" Guildis stood motionless for a moment sizing up this woman, but the steely look in her eyes told him she really did want to kill him, so he laid the knife on the bed and put his hands behind his head. Robin and her partner came running into the room and the male detective handcuffed the suspect and led him to the front door. Robin said, "You had every right to kill that piece of shit, why didn't you?" Lissa thought for a second and replied. "I want him to remember every day of his miserable life that it was ME who captured him. He can't remember if he is dead!"

Kenton County Police transported the suspect to the Kenton County Jail and told the jailers he had raped a cop and should receive preferential treatment while awaiting extradition back to Ohio to stand trial. The jailer smiled and said that they would house him in the fag unit where all the gurls could check out his manhood. That is, if they didn't shank him first. At his extradition hearing the following day, Guildis' bond was set by a Judge at three million dollars cash, after which Guildis waived extradition and was taken back to Ohio by Robin and her partner.

Robin told Lissa to make sure she attended the arraignment in Hamilton County which would be scheduled for nine o'clock a.m. to assure that the monkey got a high bond and would not be getting out of jail. At the hearing, Robin grabbed the Assistant prosecutor and introduced her to Lissa, telling her that Lissa was a law enforcement officer from Kentucky. Guildis' public defender asked for a reasonable bond, to which the prosecutor jumped out of her chair and told the Judge that the victim was in the Court and would like to address the Court. Lissa entered the secured area of the Court immediately setting off the metal detector. She smiled sheepishly and waved her badge into the air, causing the two bailiffs in the room to relax. The Judge looked down from the bench and asked Lissa where she was employed. Lissa replied, "I am an investigator for the Kentucky

Attorney General's Sexual Assault Task Force, your Honor." The Judge got a wry smile and said, "I've heard enough, bond is set at one point five million. Should the defendant make that bond, he will be required to wear an ankle monitor until trial."

***

When Lissa returned to the office, she found a message for her to call the London, Kentucky Police Department as soon as she arrived. Her call was directed to an Assistant Chief who told her that they had a ten-year-old male child who appeared to have been sexually abused, but that they were having no success in getting him to talk to them. They would keep him in protective custody until Lissa could get there to try to interview him.

Lissa drove home to pack a bag and then make the one hundred forty mile trek to the southern end of the commonwealth. By the time she arrived, it was too late to talk to a child, so she checked into a hotel and then went out for dinner. After dinner, she went to the PD to read the reports on file and to schedule a time and place for her to talk to the child the next morning. The reports offered little information other than an informant had given information about a long-term abuse of the young boy and that a Children's Services worker said the child had an understanding of sexual conduct that was well beyond his years. The meeting was set up at the County Children's Service office. When Lissa walked into the children's play room, she saw a young blonde hair boy sitting on the floor playing with a train set. Lissa had locked her sidearm in her trunk so that she would not scare the child.

She sat down on the floor near him and said, "Hi, my name is Melissa. What is your name?" The boy softly replied, "Donny." Lissa knew that she need to choose her words carefully in trying to get the child to open up to her. She saw a stuffed animal on a nearby chair and slid over to pick it up. Rather than give it to the boy, Lissa slid back to her original position and hugged the bear tightly. She saw that the boy was now intently focused on her and the stuffed bear she was holding.

Lissa looked at the boy and said, "You know, I had a man hurt me in my private parts and the only one I could talk to about it was my stuffed panda." The young boy asked meekly, "What is your panda's name" and Lissa replied, "I call her Cuddles. Do you have any stuffed animals at your house, Donny?" When the boy shook his head to indicate that he did not, Lissa asked, "Who do you have at home with you then?" Donny said his mom and two little sisters lived in their house. Lissa looked at the stuffed bear and then Donny and said, "Don't you think we should give this bear a name?" A smile came to Donny's face and Lissa continued, "Why don't you give the bear a name? And do you want it to be a boy or a girl bear?" Donny thought for a moment and looked up at Lissa and said, "I want it to be a girl bear because men scare me."

Lissa said, "Why do men scare you Donny?" She saw tears begin to flow from the boy's face as he said, "They hurt me." Lissa asked Donny what he would like to eat and smiled when he asked for peanut butter and jelly crackers. Lissa jumped up and found a staff member, telling her that, if they did not have the ingredients for the request, she would go to the local Kroger store and buy them herself. As she walked back into the play room, she saw
Donny was holding the stuffed bear as tightly as he could.

She said, "Donny, I need to go to the store to buy peanut butter, jelly, and crackers for you. I will be back soon. And can you do something for me while I am gone?" Donny got a quizzical look on his face until she said, "Keep our bear safe for me." Donny nodded vigorously and tightened his grip on the bear. When she returned with the ingredients, she noticed that Donny would not put the bear down so he could eat the crackers. Lissa said, "Why don't you put the bear between us and we can both protect it while we eat." Donny carefully placed the bear so it was touching each of their legs and began devouring the crackers coated with the PB&J.

While they were eating, a woman came into the room and asked Lissa to step outside because there was a problem. Lissa got up off the floor and, as she moved toward the door, she saw Donny grab the bear and pull it close to his chest. When the room door closed, the woman said, "The child's mother is in the lobby screaming that we have to return Donny to her." Lissa walked out into the lobby and said, "Hello, my name is Melissa Harding and I am an investigator for the Kentucky Attorney General's Sexual Assault Task Force. How can I help you?" The woman screamed, "That is my son and you have no right to keep him from me. I want him back and I want him back NOW!" Lissa calmly said, "We have reason to believe that your son may have been the victim of sexual assault and, until that issue is resolved, we have every legal right to keep him here. If you create a disturbance, you are not going to do any of your children any good from a jail cell."

The woman began screaming, "Who the fuck do you think you are you bitch?" Lissa glared back and said simply, "I am the bitch that is gonna throw your sorry ass into a cell.
Is that what you want?" The woman turned and stormed out of the center.

Lissa walked back into the play room and saw the boy still holding the bear. She said, "Why don't you keep the bear with you and protect him. I will come back tomorrow and we can talk and play some more. Would that be okay with you?" Donny smiled and said, "I would like that." As she turned to leave, Lissa said, "If anything scares you, tell someone here to call me and I will come right over."

Lissa drove back to the PD to brief the Assistant Chief, who was sitting in his office. She sat down and said, "There is no doubt in my mind that Donny has been abused. He told me that men hurt him, but did not give any details. I will stay here as long as it takes to get him to open up to me. I had a confrontation with the mother at the children's center and I really want to go talk to her." The Chief, who had been on the job over thirty years, said, "Take a uniform officer with you, and tell us anything you need to solve this. I have a grandson that boy's age, and I want to rip someone's throat out right now." The Chief picked up his phone and ordered the dispatcher to have a unit respond to the station for a call.

The Chief looked at the young officer and said, "Take Melissa to this address and stay with her. You will do whatever she tells you to do and keep your mouth shut.

Do you understand?" The officer looked quizzically at Lissa and then said simply, "Yes sir, I understand." The two quietly rode in the marked cruiser to the residence of Donny and his mother. The small house was located at the dead end of a dirt road just outside of the City limits of London. They pulled up in front and saw car parts strewn all over the yard and two young girls playing. The girls were not wearing any shoes and their plain dresses were tattered and dirty. They walked up onto the wooden porch and the uniform knocked on the front door announcing loudly, "POLICE, open the door!" The woman who answered the door was the same one with which Lissa had the confrontation at the Children's Center, so Lissa knew they had the right house.

Lissa said, "I have some questions for you. Do you mind if we come inside?" The woman glared at the two and asked, "What happens if I refuse?" Lissa shot a glare back and said, "You go to jail for Child Endangering and I call Children's Services to come pick up your girls." The woman stepped away from the door and the two cops entered. She led them to the living room where there were clothes strewn everywhere, but the house was clean.

Lissa said, "Are you married?" The woman looked down at the floor and responded, "Yes, but the low life piece of shit left me almost a year ago. I haven't heard from him since." Lissa next asked, "How do you support yourself and your family then?" The woman responded, "I work full-time at a nursing home as a nursing assistant." Lissa then asked, "Who watches your children while you are at work?" The woman responded, "My brother comes over and watches them." Lissa asked, "What is your brother's name and where does he live?" Her reply, "Bud Grant and he lives here in London on West Street."

Lissa looked into the woman's eyes and said, "There is not a doubt in my mind that Donny has been the victim of sexual abuse and I damn sure am going to find out who is doing it. If I find out you lie to me about anything, I am going to bury you in the penitentiary. Am I making myself perfectly clear?" When the woman did not answer, Lissa said, "Are there any other men who come here when Donny is here?"

The woman shot a glare at Lissa and replied, "I would never bring any men here with my kids here. I am not that kind of woman." Lissa told the woman, "If I have any more questions, we will come back. Thank you for your cooperation." When the two got back into the cruiser, Lissa said, "We now have a suspect. All we have to do is build a case. I will get the child to open up. I just don't know how long that is going to take. Run the dude for criminal history and an address so I can talk to him when the time is appropriate." The young cop replied simply, "Yes, ma'am."

Lissa was dropped off at the PD and got into her own car to go back to the hotel. She updated her case file at the hotel and made a request that she be sent video recording equipment to get her interview with the child on tape.
Within minutes she received a response saying that the
State Police would deliver what she needed the next day.

Lissa got up and showered before going to talk with Donny. She noticed that her pregnancy was beginning to show. Since she still had not told her parents about what had happened, Lissa decided she would make the short trip to Tennessee as soon as this case reached a point where she could leave.

She stopped at a bakery and bought chocolate cookies for Donny and then stopped and bought two small containers of milk for them. When she arrived at the center, she asked the staff to bring Donny to the play room. When Donny walked into the room, he saw Lissa sitting on the floor with the cookies and milk sitting out. He was carrying the stuffed bear with the same tight grip as when she had last seen him. Lissa smiled and asked, "Did you give the bear a name yet Donny?" The boy smiled and said, "I call her Melissa." Lissa said softly, "Well, thank you. I take that as a compliment."

Lissa understood that she needed to move forward slowly and carefully if she wanted to extract the information she needed from this scared little child. They munched on the cookies and Lissa said, "I went by your house yesterday and saw your sisters playing in the front yard." Donny looked up from his cookie and asked, "Why did you go to my house?" Lissa answered, "I wanted to talk to your mom about any men who could possibly hurt you." Donny asked, "What did my mom tell you?" Lissa answered, "She said the only man that comes to your house is your uncle Bud. It that true?" A look of pure fear covered Donny's face as he nodded in the affirmative.

Lissa knew the time had come, so she asked, "Has your uncle Bud hurt you?"   Tears began streaming down Donny's face and he clenched the stuffed bear tighter as he nodded "yes". Lissa told Donny, "You know that the bear and I will protect you from Uncle Bud or anyone else that wants to hurt you, don't you?" The tears were flowing unabated and Lissa was unsure whether to continue to push or to wait, but she decided that it was as good a time as any.

Lissa told Donny that she had one cookie left for him and Melissa to share and that she would be right back. She walked to the reception desk to check and see if the video equipment had arrived. The receptionist pointed to a corner where a camera was mounted on a tripod with a microphone attached. She picked up the tripod and returned to the play room where she positioned it so there was a clear view of Donny's face. She turned on the camera and announced, "This is Investigator Melissa Harding with the Kentucky Attorney General's Sexual Assault Task Force. It is Thursday, April 19th at 1030 hours and is an interview with Donny."

Lissa sat back down on the floor and said, "Don't mind the camera, just ignore it. Is it okay to talk with you about Uncle Bud?" Donny looked at the camera and then at Lissa and said, "Uncle Bud might be mad at me." Lissa touched Donny's shoulder softly and said, "Uncle Bud cannot hurt you, I promise. Your Uncle Bud babysits you and your sisters. Is that when he hurts you?" Donny nodded, but Lissa said, "Donny, you need to give answers, okay? Donny said, "Yes." "How does Uncle Bud hurt you?" Tears started flowing as the child said, "He makes me put his thing in my mouth." "How many times has Uncle Bud made you do that, Donny?" The answer shocked Lissa when the boy said, "I don't know, a bunch."

Lissa asked "Can you tell me about the first time, Donny?" Donny said, "My sisters were playing out in the yard. I saw Uncle Bud drop his pants and he told me to put in my mouth or he would spank me. He shoved it into my mouth and told me to suck in like a popsicle. He made some kind of sound and then his thing shot out something that tasted terrible and caused me to choke. He pulled it out and picked me up by my hair. He told me I would learn to do it right or he would hurt my mom and my sisters. After the first time, he made me put more and more of his thing in my mouth. It actually didn't taste as bad after a while."

Lissa leaned back and wanted to vomit. The rage inside her was building with each word the child uttered and she wanted to castrate this low-life motherfucker. She looked at Donny and said, "We will get you home real soon, so you can be with your sisters and your mom. Did your mom know that this was happening?" Donny thought for a moment and said, "I don't think so." Lissa got up off the floor and turned the camera off. She looked down at Donny and said, "I will protect you from Uncle Bud and we will keep you here until he cannot hurt you."

Back at the police station Lissa played the video for the Assistant Chief. She watched intently his face as the little boy related the horrors that he had been forced to experience. After the video was completed, Lissa suggested that they take the case directly to a Grand Jury to avoid the necessity of Donny having to testify more than once. The old cop grabbed the phone and dialed the cell of the Commonwealth Attorney who said that he already had a Grand Jury impaneled and would hold them over until Lissa could get there.

Lissa played the video of the child telling his story and watched as the females in the Grand Jury cried and the males looked enraged. She was escorted out of the room while they voted and the Commonwealth Attorney walked out into the hallway with a smile and said, "You have your indictment and I can't wait to prosecute this case."

The Assistant Chief called two cops who had the nicknames of 'Football' and "Gomer' to be with her to serve the warrant. Football had played cornerback for the University of Kentucky and Gomer had a striking resemblance to actor Jim Nabors, who played Gomer Pyle on television.

Donning her raid gear, Lissa and the two cops went to the suspect's house at 333 West Street. Lissa knocked on the front door and a large frame man answered. Lissa asked if he was

Bud Grant. When the man nodded 'yes', she asked if he would step onto the porch to talk to them. In a deep growl the suspect said, "I see you needed to bring two big male cops, you spineless little bitch." The two cops both heard the clear sound of the bones of the suspect's nose break as the backhand struck him, then heard the sound of the crack as her side kick broke his kneecap. She looked at the two cops and said, "Take this piece of garbage to the hospital because the jail will probably not accept him.

Make sure to tell everyone you see that this was done by a 'spineless little bitch'." The two cops were laughing so hard that they had trouble getting handcuffs on the man who was whining about police brutality.

Lissa drove back to the hotel to check out, but decided first to call her boss in case the garbage actually did file a beef against her. She told the Chief of Investigations about the indictment and arrest and he seemed very pleased with her. She also told him she was going to take a couple of days to make a trip home, since she was close. The Chief told her to enjoy her stay and let him know when she got back into her office.

Lissa's next call was to her mom. She told mom that she was in London, Kentucky and had just completed a case and thought she would come down for a visit. Her mom sounded thrilled to hear she was coming and promised a special dinner for her. The drive down I-75 was extremely stressful because she needed to tell them all about the rape and the pregnancy.

The first person Lissa saw when she pulled in the driveway was her brother who quipped, "Hey sis, looks like you have gained some weight in your new job." Lissa shot him the 'bird' and then walked into the house. They were all sitting at the table when Lissa said, "You need to know that I got raped in Cincinnati a few months ago and that I am now pregnant." Her mother started crying and her father looked at her and asked, "Have you made a decision on what you are going to do in the future?" Lissa answered, "I am going to put the baby up for adoption. I can't handle a child at this point in my life and I really don't want the child of the man who violated me." Dad asked if they were able to catch the man who did this to her and Lissa's response was, "Cincinnati Police identified him and he was recently arrested in Kentucky. I was lucky enough to be there when he was arrested and we are waiting for his trial to begin.

Lissa's mom asked about her new job, but all Lissa would say was that she had been assigned a couple of cases and had brought them to a successful conclusion. Lissa took the family outside to see her unmarked police car, even activating the lights which lit up the whole neighborhood because it had just gotten dark. Lissa was embarrassed to see the neighbors coming out of their homes to see what the commotion was.

There was one last person Lissa wanted to see before she headed north and that was Toni Wellbrock, the first officer she had ridden with in Lafollette. She called the police department and found out Toni was working second shift that day, so Lissa got there at the start of the shift and was waiting when Toni came out of briefing. Toni was shocked to see Lissa and even more shocked to see her wearing a badge on her belt. The two went for coffee at a local diner and chatted until Toni got a call and had to leave. They hugged as they parted and Toni told Lissa, "I am so proud of what you have done. Please keep in contact."

CHAPTER SIX

Lissa walked into her office and found a subpoena for her to appear before a Hamilton County Grand Jury. The problem was that the date of appearance was three days before. In a panic, Lissa called the Hamilton County Prosecutor's Office and told the woman who answered her issue. The receptionist transferred the call to Tom Daly, the prosecutor assigned to the case who told her that he had received a call from Detective Miller who told him that his witness would be unavailable and that they had continued it until the following Tuesday. Relieved, Lissa hung up and called Robin Miller on her cell. Robin told Lissa to park in front of CIS headquarters and they would walk to the courthouse together, then have lunch after the case had been heard by the Grand Jury. When Lissa expressed concern about her inability to identify Guildis, Robin told her, "Don't worry. His DNA already identified him."

Lissa received a call from the Chief of Investigations asking if she would like to attend a sexual assault training school at the FBI Academy in Quantico, Virginia. When she replied she would love it, she was told she could either fly into Washington or drive in the state vehicle. Lissa said she would rather drive because of her pregnancy. She was told that the class would start on Monday and that she could leave on Friday and drive at her own pace. She would be staying in a dorm room at the Academy for the three days of the class and then drive back over the next couple of days. Her state credit card would cover the gas and hotel expenses for the trip.

Lissa routed the trip so that she would pass through Columbus, Ohio, Wheeling, West Virginia, Pittsburgh and Philadelphia, Pennsylvania and then north on I-95 through Washington, DC. She arrived at the Marine Base on Sunday afternoon and was surprised to have to pass through two military checkpoints to get to the Academy. When she arrived at the FBI Academy, she had to pass through another checkpoint with the FBI Police. She checked in for the class and was informed that the training would be held in the famous "Hogan's Alley." Hogan's Alley began as a walkway that federal agents would be required to walk down. Targets would pop up on both sides and the agents had to make decisions on who to shoot and who were the 'good guys.' It had morphed into a small village with paved streets, shops, and office buildings, which all served as classrooms. As Lissa walked to her class, she saw a large sign proclaiming:

"WELCOME TO HOGAN'S ALLEY

WARNING

If you are approached by a law enforcement officer, comply fully with their requests."

Her class would be on the second floor of the only office building in the village.   There was a pharmacy, motel, restaurant, and a few other small shops that she could see.

The instructor for the class was a retired FBI agent who had spent over twenty years focused on sexual assault cases. He was said to be the 'guru' of sex crimes. He opened the class by asking the room full of local and state cops from all over the country how many believed that they knew what sexual assault victims were experiencing. Four hands went up in the room, including Lissa's. The instructor humiliated each of the three other people, all males, and then asked Lissa, "And why do you think you understand them my dear. Is it because you are a female?" Lissa shot back, "No asshole, it's because I was raped and am pregnant by the sonofabitch!" The instructor stepped back from the podium to re-group and then announced,

"This is the first time in my career that someone has put me in my place, and I apologize to you. If you are willing to walk us through what happened, I am sure it would be a learning experience to everyone here." The three days flew by and Lissa understood why this man was called the 'guru'. She had also developed new contacts from as far away as San Diego, CA and Portland, ME.

***

She was getting into the late stages of her pregnancy. She was asked if she wanted to know the sex of the baby and had told the doctor she did not. Following her pre-natal guidelines to the letter, she was told that the baby appeared to be normal and healthy. As her due date neared, she became more resolved that giving the baby up was the right thing to do.

She was asked by the AG to be the feature speaker at an event he was hosting in the State Capitol of Frankfort. He wanted her to talk about being and dealing with victims of sexual assault. When she saw the size of the crowd, she was actually intimidated. She had taken a college course in public speaking, but this was a completely new experience. As she spoke to the attendees about her experience, both during the event and then her interaction with the system, she could see that the participants were hooked onto her every word. At the end of the presentation, she received a standing ovation from the crowd.

When she returned to her office, Lissa found a lab report on her fax machine from the State Crime Lab. The report said that the rape kit in the Principle case has yielded no fluid upon which DNA could be extracted. The report went on to say, "It is likely that any seminal fluid leaked from victim's anal cavity while she was walking." Knowing that that only left the victim's identification of the suspect, she decided to review all the evidence to tighten the case. She called Det. O'Donnel and asked him to send her the parking lot video from the night of the offense and, when it arrived, watched it to see if the suspect had followed the victim out the bar. She saw the victim walking out into the parking lot at twelve forty-two a.m., but did not see the suspect. She continued to watch and saw the headlights of the Ford Fairlane turn on approximately ten minutes later. She determined that meant the suspect was lying in wait for either this victim or for the first female to leave. She rewound the video and determined that the suspect had walked out into the lot and entered his car almost an hour earlier. She asked herself how the suspect could possibly know that the victim would try to walk home or whether he had intended to follow her to her home and attack her there. She wanted to be able to find the Fairlane to get a search warrant to find the victim's DNA in the back seat.

As she pondered this case, the phone rang. The caller ID said the call was from the London Police Department. She answered and the male caller said, "This is Assistant Chief Collier of the London Police Department. I just received a call from the County Jail informing me that Uncle Bud was found dead in his cell this morning. He was found by a deputy jailer lying in his bed with his penis stuck in his mouth and with his testicles cut off. The State Police are investigating the homicide, but I wanted to check with you to see if you wanted to make the trip here and personally notify Donny and his family or if you wanted us to do it." Lissa thanked the Assistant Chief for the call and told him, "I really appreciate the call and I will drive down tomorrow morning." The people in the office jumped when they heard her scream at the top of her lungs, "THANK YOU GOD, THERE IS JUSTICE!"

***

Lissa left Northern Kentucky at five o'clock in the morning to make the drive. She was cruising along on southbound I-75 when she saw red and blue lights flashing in her rear view mirror. She pulled over immediately and quickly turned on and then off the toggle switch that activated her emergency lights. The trooper cautiously approached the driver's side of her car with his hand clearly on his gun. The trooper looked into the window and asked, "Is this a police vehicle?" Lissa showed the trooper her badge and ID and asked, "What did I do?" The young trooper got a smile on his face and said, "Only ninety-two miles per hour. In a bit of a hurry this morning?" Lissa smiled meekly and told the cop she was going to London on a follow-up investigation and that she must have been daydreaming and apologized. The trooper just laughed and said, "That woke me up this morning. Have a safe drive." Lissa learned about the term 'professional courtesy'.

When she pulled up in front of Donny's house, it was a completely different place. The car parts were gone and the grass had been recently cut. Lissa saw Donny and his sisters playing in a sandbox in the front yard. The girls were wearing clean pink dresses. Donny saw her immediately when she got out of her car and ran full speed to jump into her arms. He hugged her like he would never let him go. The leap actually caused her a sharp pain as he had driven his knee into her extended belly in his exuberance. Donny dragged Lissa into the house and yelled, "Mommy, Melissa is here!"

The mother had a wary look as she walked into the living room, which was also now clean and fresh. Lissa said, "I just wanted to come by and tell you in person that Uncle Bud will not bother you ever again. The mother got a quizzical look on her face, so Lissa said, "Ben Grant was found dead in his cell yesterday." She omitted the rest of the gory details. Before leaving London, Lissa stopped at the PD and surprised the Assistant Chief when she walked into his office and gave him a "high five!" Lissa was proud that she had closed her first case.

***

Lissa was back in her office reviewing some cold cases for the Kenton County Police when a call came in. Bill O'Donnel was the caller. He said, "We have information that the suspect in our rape will be coming back from West Virginia in the next two days and I thought you might want to be in on the bust."

Lissa walked into the PD and O'Donnel was waiting for her. He told her that two detectives were sitting on the trailer and would notify him as soon as he came back. Lissa checked into a hotel to await a call. O'Donnel called the next morning and told Lissa it was their turn to stake out the trailer. He picked her up and they went to a drive-thru to pick up breakfast. They found an isolated spot where they could see the trailer and the parking spot and settled in for a long day. The long day got real short when the police radio broadcast the Fairlane turning into the trailer park entrance. The two watched the male get out of his car and unlock the door of the trailer and walk inside. O'Donnel called for two uniform cars to respond as backup, but told them not to use their lights or siren. He ordered the three uniform cops to secure the outside of

the trailer and he and Lissa walked up to the entry door each standing to one side of the door. O'Donnel pounded on the door and yelled, "AUGUSTA POLICE, OPEN THE DOOR. YOU ARE SURROUNDED!" There was a moment of silence and then the sound of a loud bang as a bullet ripped through the door. It was followed by two more rounds fired from inside as Lissa and O'Donnel dove for cover around the suspect's car. The uniform officers returned with a barrage of gunfire, blowing out the windows, and putting holes in the aluminum trailer. After about twenty seconds, Det. O'Donnel called out, "CEASE FIRE, CEASE FIRE!" The firing stopped and the silence was deafening until the suspect opened the door of the trailer and walked out with the gun in his right hand. A loud explosion from a shotgun put an end to the ordeal as the number eight buckshot ripped into the man's face and neck. He was dead before his body ever touched the ground. Two cops ran over to handcuff the limp body and Lissa went to move from her position of cover when she saw a uniformed policeman not moving on the ground behind a cruiser. She ran over and placed two fingers on the officer's carotid artery feeling a very faint pulse. She screamed out, "Officer down, get a life squad," and immediately starting rescue breathing and CPR on the downed officer. O'Donnel called for a medical unit and the Police Chief to respond telling the dispatcher, "We have an officer down and the suspect is deceased." Lissa was working feverishly on the officer when the paramedics arrived. As soon as they took over, Lissa began feeling weak and dizzy from expelling all of her breath into the officer and depriving her body and her baby of that oxygen. When she awoke, she was on a gurney with an oxygen mask covering her face. There were medics and cops standing around and all were looking at her. She removed the mask and the first thing she asked was, "How is the officer?" O'Donnel looked at her and said, "When the medics removed his shirt and bulletproof vest, they found that a bullet made it through his side in a crease not covered by the vest and it looks like the officer suffered a significant injury. The officer was taken by medical helicopter to a Cincinnati Level One trauma unit." The medic looked at Lissa and said, "We need to take you to the hospital as well." Lissa looked at the medic and said, "Not necessary, I am fine, I just ran out of breath." The medic said, "Lady, your breath probably saved the officer's life."

Lissa heard the Police Chief saying that the State Police shooting team was en route and then heard O'Donnel say, "Boss, neither Investigator Harding nor I fired a shot." O'Donnel walked over to Lissa and, with a smile, said, "The good news is that the Cincinnati media won't get here for at least an hour, and we will be long gone by then."

On the ride back to the station to be interviewed by the shooting team, not a word was spoken by either officer. A KSP Lieutenant told Lissa he was heading up the investigation and only had one question for her. He asked, "Why didn't you fire your weapon?" Without hesitation, Lissa looked into his eyes and said, "Because I didn't have anything to shoot at. I never saw the suspect." She wrote a statement as to the events and was told she was free to leave.

Her drive back was spent re-living the horrific event she had just witnessed.

CHAPTER SEVEN

Lissa was sitting in the office completing a Use of Force form for her boss when she felt a cramp that caused her to scream out. She was on the floor in a fetal position when the staff came running in. A life squad was called and she was taken to St. Elizabeth Medical Center in Covington. The doctor in the Emergency Room told her she was in labor and was being transferred to the Labor and Delivery
Unit.

The staff placed her into a birthing chair. Her legs were spread wide open and strapped in to restrict movement. She felt a bit embarrassed as her vagina was totally visible to the one male and two female nurses in the room with her. She got concerned when she saw the three huddled in a corner whispering. Just then her female gynecologist walked in and the three huddled around her whispering. The Doc walked over and told Lissa, "We believe the baby has moved around to a position other than the one it needs to be in. We have two options, the first being to do a C-Section and bring the baby out through the stomach or we can try to move the baby and go ahead with a natural childbirth. It is your choice." Lissa said she wanted a natural childbirth. The doctor told her, "You will likely feel some discomfort as I move the baby around and how much resistance I get from it." Lissa watched as the nurses put long gloves on the doctor extending all the way up to her elbows. Lissa felt like her vagina was going to tear open as the doctor inserted both hands and arms all the way up to her elbows into her. She farted so loud that it actually scared her and the smell was awful, but the staff were wearing surgical masks, so they were not smelling it. The baby felt like it did not want to be relocated and kicked inside Lissa. It took almost an hour for the doc to move the baby into position. The whole time Lissa had to fight the urge to defecate and was continually farting.

The doctor told Lissa, "It is time for the baby to come out of hiding. I want you to take short fast breaths and when I tell you, I want you to push as hard as you can." Lissa began breathing short and hard and, when she was told to push, she screamed so loud that it shook the rafters. It took three tries to get the baby to come out. Lissa would later tell people that it was like dropping a bowling ball out of her stomach. When the baby was out, the doctor proclaimed, "Congratulations Mellissa, you have a beautiful baby girl!" She handed the baby to a nurse who wrapped it in a blanket and then looked at Lissa and said, "We are going to need to keep you in the hospital for a few days as there is significant tearing in your vaginal cavity which will require stiches. I am going to give you a sedative so that you can sleep and heal.

Lissa woke up feeling like she had ridden a camel for hundreds of miles. The nurse came into the room and asked if she would like to see and feed her baby. Lissa nodded and the nurse left and returned with the girl wrapped in a blanket. Lissa held the baby and lifted her toward her chest. She was surprised at how fast the baby attached to her swollen nipple and sucked out her breast milk. After she had enough, the baby immediately went back to sleep and Lissa handed the baby back to the nurse who asked, "Have you decided a name for her yet?" Lissa looked at the nurse and said, "I decided to allow the adopting family to choose a name. It will give them ownership of her. This baby is the result of my being raped and I want this child to grow up in a loving environment." The nurse looked into Lissa's eyes which were tearing up and said, "You have much more guts than I ever would have and I understand completely.

***

Lissa was still home recovering after two weeks when she got a call from Robin telling her, "The sonofabitch was indicted on Rape, Felonious Assault, and Aggravated Burglary and the Judge denied his request for a reduced bond. There is a pre-trial conference coming up and then a trial date will be set."

Paul Guildis and his public defender sat across from Judge David Wissman in the Judge's chambers. Judge Wissman looked at the Assistant Prosecutor and asked, "Has the State offered any kind of deal to the defendant in this case?" The young prosecutor replied, "No your Honor, we have not been able to confer with the victim for her permission and I am not authorized to make any offers until I talk to her. The Judge looked at Guildis and said, "He may not be able to offer a deal, but I can. If you take this case to trial and found guilty, I am prepared to hand out the maximum sentence allowed by law to each charge and make the sentences consecutive so that you must complete one sentence before the second one starts. If you plead to the three charges in the indictment, I will sentence you to fifteen years on the rape and make the other sentences concurrent, meaning that they will all be served together. Talk it over with your lawyer and let me know what you decide." Guildis looked at the Judge and said, "I don't need to talk to my lawyer, I ain't doing fifteen years!" The public defender looked at the judge and said, "Your Honor, let me talk it over with my client and I will let you know." The hearing was over and the Judge called the Bailiff in to return Guildis to jail.

***

Lissa finally felt good enough to return to work. She walked into her office which was full of flower and fruit baskets. They had been purchased by the AG and the staff of the Commonwealth Attorney. She had a huge smile on her face when the Commonwealth Attorney himself walked into her office and sat down. He said he needed her help on a case that Kenton County Police had going. He told her that a uniformed officer picked up a Hispanic woman walking down an isolated country road late at night. She spoke no English and is an undocumented immigrant, but investigators feel that there is a lot more to her story. He asked that she visit the woman. He told Lissa that there was a Spanish interpreter waiting at the jail for her.

Lissa walked to the jail which was less than a block from the County building. She showed the jailer her badge when she walked in but forgot that she was wearing her gun, setting off the metal detector. She smiled sheepishly and backed out of the machine, placing her weapon in a locker and removing the key. She was escorted to an interview room where the interpreter introduced herself as Sylvia Morano. There was a young woman sitting in a chair and Lissa walked around and sat behind a desk in the room. She looked at the young woman and asked, "Hablas inglais?" The young woman shook her head no and Lissa looked at the interpreter and said, "Okay then, I guess we will just call I.C.E. and start deportation proceedings." As she said that, Lissa was intently watching the young woman and could tell from the reaction that she had understood every word.

Lissa looked at the young woman and said, "You understood every word I said. Now, if you want to play stupid, then I am prepared to deal with that. If you want to let me help you, you are going to need to be honest with me. Do you understand?" The young woman nodded that she understood, so Lissa continued by asking, "How old are you really?" The young woman, in a very soft voice answered, "Sixteen." Lissa next asked, "What is your real name?" The girl answered, "Maria Santangelo." "And where are you from Maria?" "Ecuador," she answered. "How did you get to the United States, Maria?" Tears were now flowing down the girl's face as she said, "Men took me from my home after they shot and killed my father.

They put me in the back of a truck with many other women and drove us to the border. They put us in a boat late at night and we crossed into the United States. We were then put in the back of a trailer and brought here. They took us to a house and we slept on mattresses on the floor guarded by two hombres who had MS-13 tats on their arms. There was a third man who was white. He would tell us who we were going to have sex with each night and arrange to get us taken to and from the place where we would meet the men."

Lissa thought to herself, they were right. There is much more to this story. She looked at Maria and said, "We are going to get you out of here real soon and get you somewhere where you will be safe. Maria looked into Lissa's eyes and knew that she meant what she said. She said simply, "Muchas gracias, senora."

Lissa returned to the office and updated the Commonwealth Attorney telling him, "We are going to need to involve the Feds in this as it appears to be a Human Trafficking case. We also need to get her out of the adult jail as she is only sixteen years old." The
Commonwealth Attorney picked up the phone and told the Kenton County Police to get the girl from the jail and take her to a safe house that the County had. He also ordered them to assign a female officer to protect her at the safe house. He told Lissa, "You will be able to continue to talk to her there."

Lissa knew that she had to build trust quickly or the girl would escape at the first available opportunity. Lissa picked up food for both of them and, knowing that she had to start somewhere, asked, "Maria, how did you come to be on the road where you were found?" Maria said, "I was taken to a house on that road to have sex with a man. The man was extremely fat and wanted me to suck his little dick. I put it into my mouth and then bit it and ran out the front door. I didn't know where I was going, but I knew that I had to get away." Lissa asked. "Would you show me where the house is? We will protect you." Maria nodded 'yes' and Lissa returned to the office to set it up.

With a female County detective, the three rode out to where Maria was picked up and she showed them the house which was at 221 Countryside Drive. They drove Maria back to the safe house and Lissa went back to the office to have the Commonwealth Attorney draw up a search warrant. With the search warrant in hand and three members of the County Police Department, Lissa went to the house. A male member of the team knocked on the front door and yelled, "County Police, we have a search warrant. Open the door." A male voice inside said, "It's open, come on in." The four cops had their guns drawn as they entered the home and walked into the living room where an obese man in his forties was sitting on a broken down couch. A male cop asked, "You have any weapons, moron?" The man lazily looked up and said, "Don't you call me a moron and the answer to your question is NO. What is your problem?"

Lissa walked over to the man and said, "Here is the deal. You are looking at thirty years for statutory rape of a sixteen-year-old girl and when we are done with you the Feds will have a cell awaiting you for Human Trafficking. Does that answer your question?" The fat man looked her in the eye and said, "I had no idea she was sixteen. They told me she was nineteen. I can't go to jail because I have medical issues and am dying. Tell me how I can help you and I will." The obese man told the cops that he called a number whenever he wanted companionship and that a woman would be delivered to him for two hours of service. He said that it cost him $150 of his pension for this service. Lissa asked how the women were brought to him and he told her that he didn't know because he had difficulty moving off the couch and the front door was always unlocked. Lissa looked at the poor mass of fat and said, "You are under arrest, you piece of shit. Someone call for a van to take this garbage to jail where I can interview him further." They had to call an ambulance to place him on a gurney for transport to the County Jail. He was crying like a baby when they loaded him into the medic unit.

***

Upon returning to her office, Lissa had a voicemail from Robin. The message said, "Guildis accepted a deal to plead guilty to all the charges. He will be sentenced to fifteen years in prison next

Tuesday and I thought that you might want to be present at the sentencing. Let me know." Lissa called Robin and said, "I wouldn't miss it for the world. I'll meet you at C.I.S. and we can go together.

Lissa went back to the safe house with some new clothes for Maria to wear. Maria hadn't had new clothing in years and cried and smiled. Lissa asked, "Maria, how did you get to and from the places that you went?" Maria answered, "One of the men would put me in a van and take me there and then come back and get me when my time was up." Lissa asked, "Do you any idea where it is that you were staying?" The girl said that she did not. Lissa asked if Maria remembered any landmarks that they passed and Maria answered, "I was always blindfolded when they took me from the house and the blindfold was taken off when I got to the place where the man was." She continued, "There was one thing about it, the trip to the man was always much shorter than the ride back." Lissa took that to mean the driver was making sure that he was not tailed to their place.

Lissa went to the County Jail and had them wheel the fat man into an interrogation room. She looked at this poor bastard and said, "Maybe there Is a way that you can get out of this mess you have made for yourself. How often do you call for a woman's companionship?" The man said he received eight hundred dollars a month in disability, so only twice a month. Lissa said, "Then you are due for a visit. We will get you home and you will call for a woman to come and service you." The man said, "I will do whatever you tell me that I have to. I don't want to spend any more time in this shit place!"

Two detectives were inside the house while Lissa and three more detectives were outside in unmarked cars. A white van pulled up in front of the fat man's house and a bulky Hispanic man got out of the driver's seat. He walked around to the side of the windowless van and opened the side door. A young brown hair Hispanic woman, wearing a short skirt and halter top got out and walked toward the door. The driver stood and watched the woman go inside the house and then got back into the van. One of the detectives jumped on the radio and said, "Hey guys, the van has expired California plates." The supervisor called for a marked unit to make a traffic stop on the van after it got away from the house, and told the officer not to arrest the driver unless he had a murder warrant out on him.

Emilio Guterez was a twenty-two-year-old who had been recruited by MS-13 at age fourteen. He looked in the side mirror just as the red and light beacons from the cruiser lit up. Emilio glanced downward where he had a gun jammed into the seat, but had been told not to get into a gunfight with cops. His homies would get him out of jail if something went bad. The officer approached from the driver's side and said, "Good evening, sir. I am Officer Connor from the Kenton County Police. The reason that I stopped you is because your California license plates are expired. May I please see your driver's license, registration, and proof of insurance?" Guterez handed the officer his California driver's license and slowly reached toward the glove box for the registration and insurance card. He handed them to the officer who said, "I need to check to see if there are any warrants out on you. If there are not, I will write you a warning ticket. What brings you to Kentucky from California?" Emilio said, "I am here for a few months working on a construction site in Florence." The officer said, "Is there anyone else in the van right now?" When Emilio shook his head 'no', the officer said, "Mind if I look since I can't see inside?" Emilio thought about reaching for the gun, but changed his mind and opened the driver's door and got out. The officer made a cursory glance inside the back of the van and placed a GPS tracking device on the back side of the driver's seat. The officer thanked the driver and told him to get back into the van while the officer wrote the warning ticket. When the officer returned he said, "I hope that you have some other way to get to work until you can get a sticker mailed from California. Emilio assured the officer that he had other transportation, invaluable information for the investigation.

Back at the house the two detectives almost gave their position away when the young woman unzipped the fat man's pants and giggled saying, "It is so leetle!" They wanted to vomit as she performed oral sex on him and wanted to kill him as he grunted when he shot his load. The woman waited patiently for him to reload, then performed oral sex again. He handed the woman three fifty dollar bills and she walked to the front door for her ride to pick her up. Emilio pulled up in front of the house right on the two hour timeline and the detectives watched her hand him the cash as she got into the rear of the van. With the GPS tracker, they could give him a lot more leeway to get to wherever he needed to go.

Keeping a safe distance, the two undercover cars watched as the van drove in circles, going so far as to park in a WalMart parking lot for twenty minutes. The van finally reached its destination which was a farm on U.S. 25 south of Florence. The road entrance to the property had signs saying 'Electrified Fence' and 'No Trespassing'. Lissa called the State Police on her radio and asked that the State Police Helicopter to do a flyover of the property. The two cars of detectives parked their cars. Using the helicopter's FLIR infrared heat sensing technology, the pilot reported the heat signature of at least twelve people in the farmhouse. He could not locate any heat signature from any vehicles, which was surprising since the van had been back less than one hour. It was decided to put a new team on the entrance and call it a night. Lissa asked the pilot to make a daytime fly by the next morning and to get pictures of the property.

***

Lissa went into the office and immediately called her boss. She suggested that it was time to involve the Feds because they had more resources to draw from and the case apparently ran out of California. The AG told her she would be receiving calls from the FBI and ICE within the hour. A meeting was hurriedly set up bringing the Kentucky State Police, FBI, ICE and the Kenton County

Commonwealth Attorney where the aerial photos of the property were shown. The main house was approximately one thousand feet from the roadway and there was an outbuilding behind it. County records indicated that the property was six acres and was totally fenced in. This would be difficult to breach without giving warning to the people in the house.

The GPS tracking device was probably worthless because of the notice that the van's plates were expired, so they would be using other vehicles to conduct their illicit business. Lissa suggested that Maria could give them a drawing of the inside of the house. Lissa received a call from the KSP pilot telling her, "I did a flyover and saw two guys walking around the front of the house carrying automatic rifles." The challenge and the stakes just went up with the information that Maria had supplied that there were six women in the house that made for at least six bad guys. The Feds expressed concern about the possibility of another Ruby Ridge or Waco fiasco. This was going to be a difficult operation to resolve peacefully.

***

Lissa met Robin at the CIS office to go to the sentencing of Paul Guildis. The hearing only took ten minutes and Lissa smiled and waved as Guildis was led out of the courtroom in handcuffs to serve his fifteen-year sentence.

The two went to lunch and Robin said, "We are getting ready to start a new recruit class and you really should apply Lissa. I have no doubt that someday you could be my boss. Putting in an application for lateral entry which means that the time you have spent in your current job would carry over to the Police Department. It takes approximately five months to get through the process of becoming a Cincinnati cop, so your current investigations will not suffer."

After they parted, Lissa drove to City Hall and picked up the application packet to become a Cincinnati cop. She loved her current job, but the reason she moved north was to become a cop. She was torn as to what she should do.

_***

The FBI had taken the information gained from the meeting and alerted the San Diego, California office of the information garnered from the traffic stop on Emilio Guterez. They set up a stakeout on the house and determined that it was a base of operation for the MS-13 gang bangers. They brought DEA into the mix and this was developing into a major investigation.

Each trip to deliver a girl to a John was tracked by KSP and Kenton County investigators. Using the KSP chopper, officers were able to follow the movements of the traffickers without detection. It was determined that they had a total of four different vehicles at their disposal and got photos of all of the women being held captive in the house. The women appeared to range in age from fourteen to twenty and Lissa made it clear that she wanted to take down the Johns as well as the traffickers.

***

After a lot of consternation and thought, Lissa completed the application and dropped it off at

Cincinnati City Hall. When she arrived home from work, she found a message from the Cincinnati Civil Service Commission that she had been accepted as a lateral entry officer, meaning that she would not be required to take the written examination, but would have to complete all of the other phases of testing before she would be offered a position.

The first phase of the testing would be the physical agility. She was told to report to the   Cincinnati Police Academy at nine o'clock a.m.   When she arrived there were three other applicants to take the test with her. Two instructors, who were brothers, told the four that they would be running one and a half miles in less than nine minutes and then completing situps, chin-ups and push-ups. If they completed that phase, they would go through the obstacle course and would have to complete it in less than ninety seconds. They were given ten minutes to stretch out and the brothers told them to pace themselves for the run or they would not likely be able to complete the test.

The four began the run and Lissa completed the first of the six laps in just over sixty seconds, which translates into a four-minute mile. The brothers yelled for her to pace herself, but Lissa had her mind set on setting a record. As she entered the fourth lap, she had already lapped two of the other applicants and still was not breathing hard. As she started her final lap, she thought about wind-sprinting, but feared she would tire out before she completed the other phases. She ran the course in six minutes and fortytwo seconds. While one brother stayed with the other three, the other took Lissa to a bar seven feet off the ground. She was told that she needed to do ten pull-ups in under ten seconds. As Lissa did the tenth, she felt her arms tighten from the stress. They moved to the grass where she was told she needed to complete twenty-five situps in under thirty seconds. She was relieved to hear that it took her only twenty-eight seconds for her to finish. Next she was told to do twenty push-ups in twenty-five seconds. Upon completion of that task, she was told she could rest until the other three were done.

In the final phase of the testing, Lissa was outfitted with a police gun belt with cement blocks simulating a gun and a portable radio. She would be required to run fifty feet, then climb a six foot high fence, then crawl through a window and then run back to the starting line. One of the instructors showed the four how to successfully complete the test before the applicants had to complete. The first one chosen was a male who had difficulty fitting through the simulated window and took ninety-two seconds. The instructors told him that they were sorry, but he failed the test and would not be moving forward in the process. The second, also a male, tripped climbing the fence and was also eliminated. Lissa was next and completed the exercise in eighty-nine seconds. The last applicant, also a female, completed her test in eighty-two seconds and received a "high-five' from the other applicants.

The successful two were told they would be notified of the date of the physical examination.

***

 Lissa went home for a shower and then went into the office. A note was on her desk to see the Commonwealth Attorney. She walked down the hall into his office and saw him smiling. He said the San Diego office of the FBI, in conjunction with DEA, had gained enough information to raid the San Diego operation. They would be ready to take down the operation here as well. It would be a nighttime raid and there would be support from an FBI SWAT team as well as the

Kentucky State Police and Covington Police SWAT team. The Feds had obtained a Federal Search Warrant. The briefing would be at nine-thirty p.m. in the Wal-Mart parking lot, approximately a mile and a half away. He thanked Lissa for all of her work and said that he would be sending a letter to the Attorney General reflecting his appreciation. He told Lissa she was welcome to be a part of the raid if she wanted to. She looked in his eyes and said, "There is nothing I would like more."

When Lissa pulled into the parking lot she saw three armored vehicles, no less than ten marked cars and about fifty cops standing around. The FBI SWAT team commander led the briefing. Uniform officers would surround the outside perimeter of the property, the FBI SWAT team would enter from the front and the other SWAT teams would go over the back fence and hit the house from the rear. Once the house was secured, the detectives would be able to enter and search the property. There would also be air support from the Kentucky State Police. They would employ cell phone jamming equipment to stop any calls as there would be a simultaneous raid in San Diego and the power to the farm was to be cut off to stop the electric fence. The commander reminded everyone that once the power was cut, the bad guys would likely prepare for an all-out war. They would be unable to employ distraction devices because of the risks to the hostages, so everyone needed to be patient and hope that this could be resolved without bloodshed.

The first wave of tactical officers walked in from the front and the rear as soon as the power was cut. Once they had the house surrounded, the APVs rolled down the drive back to the house. A negotiator, speaking in English and then repeating in Spanish, announced, "This is the FBI. We have the house surrounded. Throw out your weapons and walk out the front door with your hands where we can see them!" The inside of the house was eerily quiet, but the helicopter detected movement in the house on the FLIR. Portable high intensity lights on one of the APVs was activated making it look like daytime. Movement about the inside of the house was visible through the windows, but there appeared to be no signs of surrender. Lissa was positioned with the other detectives wearing her bulletproof raid vest. She looked around at the firepower present and felt like this could all go to shit in less than a heartbeat. She watched in awe of the precision of the tactical operation. She heard a call on the radio from the Covington team in the back. They had seen a candle in a room and had located all of the women who were not being guarded. They told everyone they were going to breach the window and secure the hostages. There was a sound of glass breaking and then a single gunshot. The Covington team yelled into the radio that it was them who fired the shot taking out one of the bad guys. They removed the women, one by one through the broken window without any interference from the rest of the gang members inside. The negotiator yelled though the loud speaker, "You just lost your bargaining chips, give up now or you will not like the outcome." After several minutes of silence, the front door opened and the first came out the door with his hands pointing straight up in the air. That was followed by another, then another, until five males had come out. These were people who knew the drill. When each reached the grass, he would lay face down and fully extend his arms out to his side.

As the last one came out, the negotiator yelled, "Hey hombre, anyone else in the house?" The man yelled back, "Just the one you capped." Both the front and rear doors came off their hinges simultaneously as the battering rams hit them. Except for the dead male sprawled in a doorway, there were no other people in the house. Once the house had been cleared, the detectives were allowed to enter.

Lissa was horrified at the conditions in the room which held the women. The stench in the room was strong even though the window had been broken and there was a breeze flowing in. A complete search found multiple full automatic assault rifles and C4 explosives. Lissa went back outside and heard the commander telling people that the San Diego raid had been even more spectacular. Agents found twelve Hispanic women, sixty kilos of uncut cocaine, two million dollars in cash, and a cache of weaponry including military rocket launchers. With the understatement of the century, the senior agent said, "All in all, not a bad day."

CHAPTER EIGHT

Lissa showed up at the CIS office for her polygraph examination and found Robin waiting for her. Robin pulled her off to the side and told her, "The polygraph operator that you were unlucky enough to draw is a real piece of shit. The only reason he is still here is that his wife told him the day that he retires, she will kill him. Whatever happens, don't let him get under your skin. He wants to make life as miserable as possible because of his miserable existence." Robin told Lissa to wait in the waiting area and told the desk officer to call Specialist Dan Agostic and tell him his applicant was here. Agostic came to the front looking like a slob. The shirt he was wearing looked like it had been dragged for blocks on the rear of a car and the tie definitely required an oil change.

Agostic took Lissa back to a room with a desk and two chairs. He sat behind the desk and tried to devise a way flunk this bimbo and get her tossed off the list. He told her, "Every question you will be asked requires a "no" answer. If the answer to any question is "yes", then I will adjust the question until you can answer "no". Do you understand?" Lissa nodded that she did and Agostic continued, "Because you have been a law enforcement officer, there are an additional set of questions that I am required to ask. Let's begin with those." Agnostic smiled as he asked, "Have you ever had sex on duty?" Lissa said "no." Agostic next asked, "Have you ever had sex in a police car?" Lissa glared into the polygraph operator's eyes and said, "Duh, if I answered no to the first question, I doubt that I would go find a police car to have sex in!"   Agostic wrote "no" for the answer and then moved on to his next question, which he loved to ask because it made people squirm.   He asked, "Have you ever been involved in a strange sex act?" Lissa leaned back and said, "I guess the answer to that question is yes, if you consider being raped a strange sex act."   Agostic asked, "When were you raped?" Lissa answered, "A little over a year ago in downtown. I just appeared at the sentencing where the piece of shit rode off into the sunset to serve his fifteen years in the Ohio Penal System." Agostic's last question was, "Is everything on your application true and accurate?" Lissa thought for a moment and said, "I'm not sure. The application asked if I had any children and I answered "no." I got pregnant with the rapist's baby, but I gave it away as soon as she was born. So you tell me whether I falsified the application?"   When they were done with the lie box, Lissa looked at Agostic and said, "You don't need to escort me out. I know this place as well as you do."

***

Lissa arrived back at the office and opened her e-mails to catch up on work. The first was a forward from the AG. It was sent by the supervising agent of the Cincinnati office of the FBI. It read:

> On behalf of Director Comey and Attorney General Holder, I would like to express our deep gratitude for

the efforts of your investigator, Melissa Harding. Other than the raids that you are aware of, we were also able to conduct raids in Dallas,

Seattle, Denver, Philadelphia, Memphis and Kansas City. Those raids netted seizures of cash and property valued at over ten million dollars. A percentage of those seizures will be coming to your office for use in furthering your law enforcement efforts. Please thank her for a job well done.

A note attached from the Kentucky Attorney General said simply,

"Melissa, you are a great asset to this agency. Thank you for your service and efforts."

Lissa printed a copy of the e-mail and mailed it to her parents.

***

Lissa received a letter from the Cincinnati Police stating that she was scheduled for the psychological portion of the applicant process. Dr. Jim Don was an independent psychologist who specialized in law enforcement officers.

The first part of the testing was a written test called the

MMPI2, a test which Lissa learned about while in college. The test measures the socialization skills and well as the truthfulness of the applicant and consisted of five hundred and sixty questions. She knew from college that the same question was asked four different ways to see if it generated a consistent answer. It took her almost two hours to complete. The written test was followed by the interview portion with the doctor.

Lissa felt totally relaxed as soon as she met Doctor Don. He seemed soothing and gentle. They chatted about her life and then into her career. Dr. Don asked, "Have you ever been involved in a lethal use of force Melissa?" Lissa thought for a moment and replied, "Yes and no. I was in a shootout involving a rape suspect, but I did not personally fire any shots." Dr. Don followed up with the same question asked by the KSP commander, which was "Why didn't you fire?" Lissa answered, "I am going to give you the same answer that I gave to investigators who asked that exact question. I did not fire because I did not see a target to fire at. Cops shot up the trailer and I was ducking behind the cover of a car when he came out the front door. A shotgun blast dropped him like a bag of rocks before I could raise my gun to fire." Dr. Don's follow-up to that was, "How did you feel after you saw the man get shot?" Lissa paused for a second and said, "The only feeling that I remember having was one of relief that it was over. I felt nothing for the dead guy. He chose his own path of destruction." Dr. Don smiled at her and said, "You will be hearing from the Civil Service Commission in a couple of weeks with where you stand.

I wish you great success in your career. It was a pleasure to meet you."

As she walked out of the doctor's office, her cell phone rang. The Chief of Investigations told her that the University of Kentucky Police in Lexington requested the office's assistance with a date rape case they were investigating. Lissa said she would head home to pick up clothes and make the seventy-five mile drive in an hour.

Lissa walked into the Police Department on the University of Kentucky and was taken directly to the Chief's Office. The Chief was a man who appeared to be in his early thirties and Lissa thought he was awfully young to be a Chief. Chief Tim Williamson had gotten his Master's Degree in Police Administration by the time he was twenty-three. He had an athletic body and had played college baseball at Penn State University. He turned down a contract to play professional baseball to be a police officer at Temple University in Philadelphia. While at Temple, he had received his Ph.D. in criminology and had been at UK less than one year.

The Chief said, "I have heard great things about you, Ms. Harding. The reason we called in the task force is because something about this case just doesn't smell right. The victim has changed her story multiple times and my investigators are having difficulty verifying anything she has said. We asked her to take a polygraph, but she declined. My investigators are at your disposal. Anything you need, they will get you. If they can't get what you want, see me because I will get it for you."

Lissa asked for the file of the case to take back to her hotel room to review. She asked the Chief to set up an interview the next day with the victim and to tell the victim that the meeting would be at any place she wanted. She left the campus with the file and checked into a Marriott nearby.

After reading the report and investigative summary, Lissa agreed that something just did not add up. The victim claimed to have attended a frat party at the Beta Tai Alpha fraternity house on a Friday night, but that fraternity had its privileges suspended for a week for a hazing incident and Campus Police had made five separate checks that night to assure that the suspension was being honored.

Those checks included the officer walking around the house to verify.

Lissa went to the Health Services Office of the University of Kentucky to meet with the victim, an eighteen-year-old freshman named Dorothy Dumatta. Dorothy hailed from a small Tennessee town north of Nashville and Lissa would use her Tennessee roots to endear herself to the victim. Dumatta was in the waiting area when Lissa arrived. Lissa told the victim that they would be in a private office in the Center.

They sat in the office and Lissa said, "My name is Melissa Harding and I am an Investigator for the Kentucky Attorney General's Sexual Assault Task Force." The campus police requested our assistance in catching the person or people who did this to you. I want to start by telling you that I know exactly what you are experiencing because I was raped in Cincinnati, Ohio last year. We just sent the bastard who did this to me away for the next fifteen years. Can you tell me what happened?"

There were tears flowing as Dorothy began telling the story. "A girl friend suggested we go to a frat party that night. We walked to the party and there was booze and pot being smoked everywhere. I admit that I was drinking, but I don't do grass. A black guy walked over to me and told me he was a football player for UK. He asked me if I wanted a refill for my drink and said it was a bourbon and coke. The next thing I remember is waking up on a bed naked and there was blood on the sheet. I felt like someone had driven a bulldozer inside me. My clothes were in a pile alongside the bed and I put them on and ran out of the door."

The girl's eyes told Lissa that she was telling the truth, but the truth just didn't match up with the known facts. Lissa asked, "Why did you wait to call the Police?" The girl sobbed and said, "I was embarrassed and thought I might have caused it myself by the drinking. Two days later, my vagina was still real sore and I came here to the clinic, where they asked me what happened and they called the Police." Lissa thought for a second and asked, "What is your friend's name?

I would really like to talk to her too." Dorothy said, "Her name is Shirley." "What is her last name and how long have you known her, Dorothy?" Dorothy said, "Her last name is Williamson and I only met her earlier that day?" Lissa asked, "Where did you meet her, Dorothy?" She answered, "She was in the cafeteria and sat down on the other side of me. We talked for a while about school and such and then she told me about the party. Since I had only been on campus a few weeks, she told me to meet her at the cafeteria and we could walk to the party. She said that she knew a shortcut, so we went through a couple of buildings, then down a walkway, then up the street until we reached the house. We got there about ten p.m. and the party was going strong. A light bulb in Lissa's head seemed to light up and she said, "You would know the house if you saw it, wouldn't you?" Dorothy nodded yes. Lissa said, "Let's take a ride in my car."

The two got into Lissa's state cruiser and Lissa switched the radio to UK's Police frequency. She said into the radio, "This is Investigator Harding from the Attorney General's

Office to University of Kentucky Police Communications." The male sitting at the dispatch desk looked at the female sitting at the console next to him and said, "Say WHAT????" He pressed the talk key and said, "This is the University of Kentucky Police Communication Center, go ahead with your traffic." The female at the next console looked over and said, "The Police Chief is on line 2 for you."

The male on the phone said, "This is Chief Williamson. The person using our frequency is acting on my authority. Give her anything she asks for. That means if she wants you to run down the hall and get her coffee, you are going to run down the hall. GOT IT?" The dispatcher said, "Yes, sir" and the Chief hung up. The dispatcher hit the talk button and said, "How can I be of assistance to you?" Lissa said, "I am in front of the Health Center and I need directions to the Beta Tai Alpha Fraternity House." The dispatcher keyed up and said, "Go out of the center and turn left. When you pass the School of Law you will turn right and follow that to the deadend. Make a left onto Campus Drive and turn right at the first street. The House is at 221 East Avenue, fourth house on your left." Lissa followed the directions and stopped in front of 221 East Avenue.

She looked at Dorothy and asked, "Is this the house you were raped at?" Dorothy looked at the house, then at Lissa, and said simply, "No, it is not." Lissa keyed the mike and repeated, "Investigator Harding to UK Communications." The dispatcher jumped to answer, "This is UK communications, go ahead with your traffic." Lissa said, "Would you contact the Police Chief and ask him to meet me at 221 East Avenue ASAP?" After a moment of silence, the dispatcher said, "Car 1 is en route to your location, ETA approximately six minutes." Within just a few minutes a white Ford Escape pulled up behind Lissa's car.

Lissa told Dorothy to wait in the car. Lissa walked back to the driver's door and said, "You were correct Chief, there was something wrong with this case. I have no doubt that this young girl was, in fact, a rape victim, but she says this is not the place where it took place. It occurred at a different house.

The victim says a woman she met in the cafeteria told her about the party and then took her on a circuitous route to make sure she did not know where she was. The victim was given a "mickey" and then raped on the second floor of the house. We need to get the cafeteria tape and security video to identify the woman who the victim only knows to be named Shirley Willis." The Chief smiled up from the driver's seat and said, "Damn lady, you want to come work for me?"

Investigators poured over the cafeteria video until they found Dorothy entering. They followed her through the cafeteria line and watched her sit down. A few moments passed before a young black woman sat down across from her. The investigators froze the camera and printed out a picture of the woman. They put together a photo lineup and Dorothy positively identified the woman as the one who led her to the house where she was raped. UK Police ran a facial recognition program against persons who had been processed into the Fayette County Jail and came up with a hit. The woman's real name was Chantai Davidson and she had multiple arrests in Lexington Metro area. The last known address for Davidson turned out to be a parking garage and the investigation seemed stymied.

***

Lissa opened her e-mail and saw a message from the Cincinnati Civil Service Commission. It said, "Congratulations, you have made it to the final stage of the hiring process for the Cincinnati Police Department.

You are scheduled for the Oral Interview on Tuesday at ten o'clock a.m. at the Police Administration Building located at 310 Ezzard Charles Drive. Please arrive on time as tardiness will eliminate you from the process."

Lissa already had accepted a date with a new attorney in the office to have dinner and see a Red's game, but that would not conflict with her interview.

Lissa arrived at District One headquarters with just seven minutes to spare. She walked up to the desk officer and then remembered she was still wearing her gun. She looked at the old cop, who was retiring in less than one month, and said, "Hi, I am here for the oral interview, but I have a question." She raised her badge and ID to the glass partition and asked, "I am wearing my gun. It that going to present an issue?" The veteran cop laughed and grabbed the phone. He answered, "Damned if I know." The cop pointed to the door on Lissa's left and told her to take the elevator to the third floor and turn left. He pushed the release button under his desk to unlock the door for her.

When she walked into the room, there were three men and two women seated at a table and there was one chair in the center of the room. The male on the far left of the table pointed to the chair, indicating Lissa should have a seat. As she said down, the man said, "Let me start this by introducing everyone at the table to you. I am Lt. Col.

Dave Buelly and just to my left is Lt. Col Jim Helen. Next to him is Captain Kim Fuego and next to her is Angela Davis from the Civil Service Commission. At the other end is Bishop Peterson Mongo, Pastor of the Light of the World Baptist Church. We will each ask you one question, with an option for a follow-up question beginning with me and working down the table. We will then each have an opportunity to ask one more question, if we choose. Do you understand how this is going to work?" Lissa answered simply, Yes, Sir."

Col. Buelly continued, "My question is that you seem to have a pretty good job now, so why would you want to be a Cincinnati Police Officer?" Lissa had decided that she would take one slow breath before answering any questions asked, thereby giving her time to formulate an answer. She said, "You are correct, Colonel. I have a great job and I love it, but I grew up wanting to be a police officer. The reason I chose Cincinnati is that I grew up in a town on the Tennessee and Kentucky border and Cincinnati was the closest major city with professional sports teams and a rich history. It will offer me more opportunities to advance."

Col. Helen asked, "Have you ever used excessive force in making an arrest?" Lissa answered, "The amount of force necessary to take a person into custody is solely determined by the amount of resistance offered by the person being arrested. Think of it this way. A young child is mesmerized by the flame on the burner. The child reaches toward the flame and the adult says "don't do that." As the child continues to reach his hand toward the flame the voice of the adult escalates to "DON'T DO THAT!" When the child continues to reach toward the flame, the adult screams out an order; then, when all else fails, grabs the child's arm and pulls him away. So the answer to your question is that I have never used excessive force, sir."

Captain Fuego asked, "I understand you recently had a child. Is that going to affect your ability to work different shifts?" Lissa pondered her answer and said, "Captain, I gave up my child at birth. She was not conceived out of love, but was a result of a rape. I felt that I could not give her the love that she deserved and that a loving family was best for her."

The woman from the Civil Service Commission asked, "Where do you see yourself in five years?" Lissa replied, "I have a definite plan for my future. Within three years I would like to be in a specialized unit such as canine or mounted patrol. Within five years I want to be a Sergeant or Lieutenant, and within ten I want to be a Captain."

The Bishop asked, "Do you believe there is racism in police officers?" Lissa answered, "Bishop, there is racism in all segments of society. There is racism in whites hating blacks and Hispanics, there is racism in blacks hating Asians and Hispanics, and in Hispanics hating other ethnic groups. But, to specifically answer your question, I do not believe that racism permeates within the law enforcement community."

Col. Buelly asked if anyone had any further questions and then thanked Lissa for her candor. He said, "The decision will be make within the next two weeks and you will be notified by mail. Thank you for coming." Lissa smiled and left the room.

Lissa had a fun evening with her date. Rob Duncan was just out of law school and this would be his first real job. He was friendly and outgoing. They went to the Montgomery Inn Boathouse and enjoyed their world-class ribs before going to the baseball game at Great American Ball Park. They had left their cars at the Covington office and ridden in a cab to the restaurant and then to the ballpark. After the game, they decided to just walk across the bridge to get back to their cars.

Rob told Lissa how much he enjoyed her company and maybe they could together again. Lissa thought for a very long second and replied, "I think I would really enjoy that."

***

Lissa went back to the office and called the UK Police for an update on their case. She was told that the suspect had not yet been located, but that an active search was underway to find her. Lissa decided to make the drive to Lexington to try an idea she had come up with.

Lissa met with the Police Chief and his investigators to present her idea to them. They would have the victim return to the cafeteria and hope that the suspect would see her and make contact. Lissa and the investigators would be there to protect the victim should she initiate contact. The Chief approved the plan and Lissa presented it to Dorothy, who did not appear to relish the thought. For each of the next three days, Dorothy sat at the same table and ate at the cafeteria. On the fourth day, the same black woman sat across from her and began to chat. Lissa walked over to the table and said, "Hey Dorothy, who is your friend?" Dorothy replied, "This is Shirley." Lissa sat down next to Shirley and talked about her accounting classes and how she needed a release from the stress. Shirley said, "There is a frat party on Friday, if you think you might be interested. We could meet here and I can take you there. Can you be here at eight o'clock?" Lissa smiled and said, "I don't know many people on campus

yet, so it sounds like fun. I will meet you here." When Shirley left, one of the investigators followed behind.

Lissa stood out in front of the cafeteria at eight o'clock waiting for the suspect to arrive. She had been wired so that the investigators would be able to hear and record all that was said.

Lissa was getting depressed when, at eight fifteen, no one had showed up. As they were preparing to shut down for the night, Shirley appeared. She told Lissa, "I know a shortcut we can take, since you are not familiar with the campus yet." The two walked down a sidewalk and entered a building. Lissa said, "This is my first time in the Communication Arts Building." The two exited a side door and walked down another path entering the School of Law. Lissa said simply, "I actually thought about attending Law School," telling her backup team where she was. Lissa took note that Shirley was constantly looking back to make sure that they were not being followed. A second team of campus police investigators was waiting in their car at the side entrance to the Law School and saw Lissa and Shirley exit the door onto Commerce Street. Shirley led her prey up the street to an old looking house and then up the steps to the front door. When Lissa walked into the house, there was music playing and she could smell the pungent odor of pot. Shirley pointed toward a table and told Lissa to pour herself a drink. Lissa made a bourbon and coke and then set it down and grabbed a glass that had ice in it, but had already been almost finished by someone else. She stood with the almost empty drink in her hand when a black male walked up and said hello. Lissa smiled and the man said, "I play football for the University. Can I refill that drink for you?" Lissa nodded, and when the man walked away with the glass, Lissa announced into the microphone she was wearing, "As soon as I say "thanks for the drink," hit the house." The man returned and said, "I tried not to make it too strong for you." Lissa smiled at him and said, "Thanks for the drink." Lissa stood watching the partiers when the man asked, "Aren't you going to drink it?" Lissa smiled and replied, "No, I am going to have it tested for a 'roofie." As ten cops came running in the door yelling, University of Kentucky Police, nobody move. There was a mad scramble as people tried to run out the back door, but there were cops covering that door as well. Shirley tried to escape through a window, but was tackled and handcuffed. Lissa knew that she would be the key to unlocking this mystery. Several of the partygoers were UK students who were underage. They were cited for drinking and released. The black male who claimed to be a football player, Damian Holsteiin, turned out to be a wanted drug dealer who had never attended any university other that the Eddyville State Pen where he had served five years. The drink was poured into a plastic vial to be analyzed for any foreign substance. Damian and Chantai were taken to the UK Police headquarters for questioning.

***

Chantai was sitting in a chair handcuffed to the table when Lissa walked in. Lissa said, "Let me lay this out for you so that even your feeble brain understands. The question is not whether you are going to prison, but how long you are going to be there. You can roll over on your boyfriend who is going to rot away in prison, or you can remain quiet and rot away in prison yourself. It is your choice."

Chantai glared back at Lissa and said, "You got nothing bitch. I want a lawyer." Lissa just laughed and said, "I have to stop asking questions now, but I can still talk. When the lab results of the drink come back with a date rape drug, you and the stud will both go down for felony tainting the drink and attempted rape of me. Then we will charge you with Complicity to Rape for the other woman and drop as many charges as possible on both of you. All I can say is that I hope you like interacting sexually with women for a lot of years to come. We will wait for your attorney to come." Lissa walked out of the room where she was met by the Police Chief, who was laughing. He looked at her and said, "I think you gave her a lot to think about!"

CHAPTER NINE

Lissa had just come home from work and stopped to grab her mail. There was a letter from the Cincinnati Civil Service Commission and she excitedly ripped it open. The letter said:

"This letter is to inform you that you have been selected to be a Cincinnati Police Officer. You will be entering as a lateral entry candidate with all of your law enforcement experience credited to you. The Ohio Peace Officer Training Commission, the certifying authority for training in Ohio, has declined to accept any of your prior law enforcement training, so you will need to attend the complete police academy which will begin on May 19th.

Unlike other police recruits, your probationary period will begin on the first day of the police academy and will end upon your successful completion of the training. You will also be required to have established a residence in Hamilton County, Ohio at the time of appointment. You have twenty-one days from the date of this letter to confirm your acceptance of this offer or it will be automatically rescinded. Congratulations and welcome to employment with the City of Cincinnati

Respectfully,

Cincinnati Civil Service Commission"

The elderly landlord sat in amazement looking out of her bay window watching her tenant do what can only be described as a 'happy dance'. She had no idea what would cause the young woman to be jumping up and down and waving what looked like an envelope and letter.

Lissa went inside and sat down on the couch. She knew that she would now have to make a decision on a career path. She grabbed a legal pad off the table and on the left side wrote "PROS." Then, on the right side of the pad she wrote "CONS." On the "PROS" side she wrote, "This is what I always wanted." On the "CONS" side she wrote, "I love the job I have." Next she wrote on the PROS side, "This job offers career choices." On the CONS side she wrote, "Taking this job is a risk." Next, on the CONS side she wrote, "Political appointment, job not guaranteed." Clearly this was going to be a very difficult decision.

Lissa picked up the phone and called Robin's cell. When Robin answered, Lissa said, "Hey, let's have dinner. I will buy since I need to pick your brain. Lissa said she wanted to celebrate, so she chose Ruth's Chris Steak House across from the Stadiums downtown.

The two were enjoying a glass of wine before dinner when Lissa sprung the news that she had been offered the position with Cincinnati. Looking directly into Robin's eyes, Lissa said, "I am having a really tough time trying to make a decision and hoped that you could offer some insight." Robin looked down and appeared to be in deep thought, then looked at Lissa and said, "You are right, you do have a tough call to make. I know that you enjoy the freedom in the job you have now, and you would lose that at the Police Department. I am not sure what the chances for advancement are at the place you work now, but I have no doubt that, if you join us, someday you will outrank me." Lissa brought out her PROS and CONS sheet for Robin to look at and Robin read it carefully and handed it back.

***

Lissa went on a second date with Rob. They attended a live show at the Arnoff Center in downtown Cincinnati and then went to a little hole in the wall restaurant that had been featured on Food Network for their buffalo wings. Rob picked her up and then drove her home. She decided to invite him in for a nightcap as he was a total gentleman.

They sat and chatted on her couch and then he moved to kiss her. She enjoyed the way he treated her with respect and how patient he was with her. They stood up in a long embrace and a passionate kiss, so she slid her hands down to his waist and unbuckled his pants. She lowered herself to her knees while dropping his pants to his ankles. She lowered his underwear exposing his manhood. She wrapped her lips around the head of his penis causing his erection to grow. As she tried to take him in deeper, she thought of the ten-year-old boy and Uncle Bud and began gagging. She jumped to her feet and went to the bathroom where she grabbed a hand towel off the rack. When she returned, he was standing motionless in the living room. She held the hand towel in her left hand underneath his erection and gently stroked him with her right hand. She could feel him tremble as he got closer and closer. She whispered, "Don't make it happen, just let it happen." As he tightened his muscles up, she slowed to make the feeling last as long as possible. She watched as the creamy liquid shot out onto the towel and then the fear set in on her. His pulsations from ejaculation were the same as she felt when her rapist shot deep inside her. She controlled her feelings until the pulsating stopped and then cleaned him off with the towel. She walked back into the bathroom and threw the towel in the sink to be washed.

When she returned, his pants were back up and his belt was buckled. She looked at him with passionate eyes and said, "Rob, if there was any man on this earth that I would want to have sex with, it would be you. But the man who raped me took away my ability to have sex with anyone and I cannot say that it will ever come back. I would understand if you decide not to see me anymore." Rob looked her square in the eyes and said, "I really enjoy your company and I understand that you were violated. I would love to continue seeing you, if you don't have an issue with me filling my physical needs elsewhere." Lissa thought for a moment and replied, "I can live with that arrangement."

***

Lissa sat on the couch and tried to write her resignation from her job with the Kentucky Attorney General. She would write a paragraph and then rip the sheet off the pad because it did not adequately show her appreciation for the opportunity she had been given. The final letter said:

"It is my intent to resign from my position as an Investigator with the Sexual Assault Task Force effective two weeks from today to accept a position as a Police Officer in Cincinnati, Ohio. This was an extraordinarily difficult decision as my employment with the Attorney General has been both fulfilling and rewarding. The opportunity you have given me has resulted in me maturing and loving my career choice.

What your office has offered me will surely help me protect and serve the citizens of Cincinnati. I will deliver my vehicle, weapons and identification to the Kentucky State Police at the Dry Ridge post on my final day.

> "Your trust in me can never be re-paid and I will forever be in your debt.

> Melissa G. Harding"

She would drive to Frankfort to personally deliver the letter.

Lissa called the Civil Service Commission to accept the position and was told to report one week before the recruit class started for her orientation.

She then went looking for a place to live on the Ohio side of the river. She found a quaint little house on the east side of the City in a neighborhood called Mount Lookout. It had a view of the Ohio River from the back porch and looked perfect for her needs. The owner wanted one hundred fifty thousand dollars for the house, but it needed repairs and Lissa just was not willing to pay that much. She countered with one hundred ten thousand cash, since she still had the settlement from her former employer.

They settled for one hundred twenty-five thousand and Lissa now owned a home in the City.

Lissa was sworn in as a police officer on the first day of orientation. She and the other recruits were handed their badges and administered the oath of office, swearing to enforce the laws of the State of Ohio and to uphold the Constitution of the United States. Immediately after being sworn, their badges were all taken back to be returned upon graduation.

Lissa was next measured for her grey recruit uniform and provided a tour of the police districts as well as informed about the benefit package available to cops in the City. She was invited to stop in at the FOP Lodge 69 building on Central Parkway where she was met by the current president, a female Sergeant named Kathleen Harrison. Harrison welcomed her into the Police Department and told her, "We are here to serve you." Lissa thanked her and went home to prepare for her first day of class.

The first day of class for a police recruit is filled with anticipation and intimidation. To pass under a sign that says, "The finest police officers in the country pass through these doors" sets a standard of excellence which is difficult to live up to. Listening to the Police Chief and the Academy Commander lay out the high expectations that they have is a very intimidating experience as well.

The first three weeks of the training covered things that Lissa had already covered. She was seated in class daydreaming when the instructor yelled, "Recruit Harding, I guess you learned all of this in college, am I boring you?" Lissa looked embarrassed as she replied, "No, sir. I learned this in Kentucky Police training and from experience as a law enforcement officer." The instructor looked surprised and asked, "Why aren't you in the abbreviated academy with the other cops then?" Lissa looked at him and said, "Because the State refused to accept my previous training, sir."

As they approached the tenth week, the class was told they would be assigned to a Police District for two weeks to ride with an experienced officer and see the implementation of what they had learned so far. The assignments were posted and Lissa noted that her name was not on the list. On the Friday before the two weeks started, she was taken out of class and met a Sergeant from the Central Vice Unit, who told her, "Because of your experiences already it was determined that we could better utilize you in our unit for the two weeks. Report to the Vice Control Section at ten a.m. Monday morning.

***

Lissa arrived at the Vice office and was told that the briefing was just beginning. She would be acting as a decoy for Johns seeking the services of prostitutes. She would be unarmed, but would have a four-person backup team in place to make arrests and protect her. She was shown a wardrobe room and told to pick out a sex outfit to wear. She chose a skin tight black dress and mesh panty hose along with a low cut white blouse. The vice cops let out catcalls as she walked back into the briefing room. She actually loved the attention and it made her feel welcome.

Lissa was dropped off in front of a no-tell motel called the Traveler's Inn on Central Parkway. The one vice cop said there should be a sign underneath saying, "Sheets changed by the hour," to which everyone laughed. Lissa was told that the John had to say both a sex act and an amount for a crime to have been committed. She was told he has to say, "Fucky, Sucky, five buck" or it would be entrapment. She was to tell the John to meet her in the parking lot of the motel which was above the street and the bust would occur there. She was told that her every word would be heard by her backup and recorded for evidence so she should be very careful as to what she said.

Lissa walked down to the street and stood near the corner. She had not been there ten minutes when a black Cadillac Escalade with tinted windows pulled up. The window rolled down and the black male driver, who appeared to be a large framed man, said, "You ain't one of my bitches."   Lissa glared at him and said, "I ain't no man's bitch. I don't share my take with anyone." Lissa stepped back when the door of the car opened and she could see that this was a large man. Her backup team got out of the van they were in, ready to come to her aid. The large pimp looked at Lissa and said, "This is my corner and you will be one of my bitches, understand?" He moved one step closer and Lissa's hand shot out striking the pimp in the Adam's apple and causing him to drop like a sack of potatoes gasping for air. Her backup cops stood by the van laughing and watching as the pimp floundered like a chicken gasping for air. Lissa quietly sauntered down the street to where two other hookers had taken their spot for the day. She looked at the two and said, "We should move on for a bit as this place will be crawling with cops in a few minutes. The shorter of the two, a black woman who made it clear she was not wearing panties, said, "Girl, you need to find another place. He is one bad mutha fucka!" Lissa shot a glance back at the man who was on the ground writhing in pain and said, "He don't look so badass to me." The two vice cops were rolling in laughter, but decided to call for medical aid for the poor bastard on the ground. As the sirens could be heard coming, the three women moved down the street to watch from a safe distance.

Once the pimp was removed and the Escalade towed, the three moved back to their respective spots to conduct business. It didn't take long before a van pulled up where Lissa was standing. She walked over and looked in the window at the obese man, whose pants were open and his small penis sticking out. Lissa asked, "What do you want me to do with that?" The man said, "I want you to suck it dry." Lissa next asked, "And what do I get in return?" The man replied, "What do you want to get in return?" Remembering that she could not state an amount Lissa said, "What is it worth to you for me to do that?"

The man smiled and said, "How about twenty?" Lissa smiled and said, "Deal. Drive up into the motel lot and I will meet you there." The man pulled away and turned into the parking lot. When he parked in a space, the two backup cars blocked him in and four cops jumped out of their cars wearing their badges on lanyards hanging from their necks. They ordered the man, who was in his late forties, out of the van and handcuffed him. One of the vice cops looked at the pitiful man, and with a smile said, "You have been stung!" The man cried as he told the cops that he is married and his wife would divorce him. One of the other vice guys smirked and said, "Would have been nice if you had thought about that before you solicited a cop."

The team was impressed that Lissa got six men to fall for her lines before the teams called it a day. She got an 'attaboy' from the Commander of the Unit at the end of the day.

***

With graduation nearing, the recruits were becoming anxious about the final examination which would be administered by the State. They were told that the examiners would bring the test monitor to assure no one cheated and then take the completed tests back to Columbus to be scored. They would know the results in three days.

Lissa had told her parents about the graduation date and they had promised to make the trek up to Cincinnati to be there for her. The graduation ceremony would be held at the Duke Energy Convention Center and the Mayor and Police Chief would be making the presentation. After the ceremony which took more than two hours, the recruits all threw their white hats into the air in celebration.

Lissa's brother and parents stayed at her new house, which still had not been completely furnished. Her brother was relegated to the couch because Lissa had not had the time to buy a bed for the third bedroom. Lissa made a cameo appearance at the class graduation party which was held at the Westin Hotel just to wish her classmates well and then went to dinner with her family.

When she returned to the Police Academy, the assignments of where the new class would be assigned was posted. She would be working in District One, the downtown area, on the six a.m. to four p.m. shift. Her Field Training Officer would be Officer Liza Seemoan. One of her classmates bemoaned her bad luck commenting, "Seemoan is known as 'bitchwitch' in District One because of the number of recruits she has gotten fired."

CHAPTER TEN

Lissa arrived at District One at five-thirty so she would not be late her first day. She had to use the public entrance to the station because she had not been given the code to enter the "POLICE ONLY" entrance.

Seemoan, a forty-one year old blonde woman, walked up and said, "You must be Harding, my new recruit." Lissa smiled and nodded and Seemoan said, "Don't expect special treatment just because you are also female." Lissa shot her FTO a glare that could have killed and said, "What I expect is to be treated like a probationary police officer, nothing more and definitely nothing less." Seemoan smiled and said, "I think we are going to get along great recruit."

Lissa listened intently as the Sergeant read off the beat assignments. They would be in car 1107 covering the Over the Rhine area of the District. Over the Rhine is just north of the downtown area and has transformed from one of the toughest areas in the City to a yuppie mecca, featuring upscale shops and bars. The two walked out to the car and Lissa automatically went for the driver's side. Seemoan bristled and said, "You have to earn the right to drive the police car lady." Lissa quietly moved to the passenger side and opened the door. Seemoan bristled again, yelling, "What do you think you are doing? We don't get into the car until we walk all the way around it checking for new dents and dings. The last person who had the cruiser is responsible for any damage to it. Then we check the trunk to make sure everything is in there that is supposed to be."

Once everything checked out, they pulled out of the lot to begin their patrol. Liza looked at   Lissa and said, "You are my last recruit that I will be training. The guy I had before you was a great cop until he committed suicide after his wife, who was also a cop was killed in an ambush. I am just plain burned out."

Liza told Lissa, "Here is how this will work. At the end of each shift I will evaluate you on whatever we did. Using a seven-point scale, with one being a toad and seven being superwoman, I will score you for radio procedure, appearance, report writing or whatever else we do during the course of the shift. After the first four weeks with me, you will go to a second FTO for four weeks and then move on to a third for four more weeks. The last four weeks are with me and I expect to see major improvement in all of the areas that are evaluated. Don't look for any high numbers early on, but look at the comments to see what you need to do to improve.

The recruit binder goes everywhere you go and each daily report ends up in it. You probably heard about my reputation as a bitch, but the reality is that someday you will likely back me up and I want you to be reliable."

As they rode along the streets of the area called Over the Rhine, Liza explained how the area they were patrolling had been transformed. She asked if Lissa remembered the 2001 riot in Cincinnati and said, "This is where it all began. A cop working an off-duty detail at one of the bars saw a man wanted for traffic warrants. A foot pursuit started and the suspect ran into an alley. Another officer had taken up the chase and thought the guy was reaching for a gun and capped him. The guy turned out to be unarmed and all hell broke loose in Cincinnati. The race baiters screamed that the cop shot him because he was black and they ended up charging the cop with Misdemeanor Negligent Homicide. The cop was found not guilty by a Judge. The cop had already quit his job and became a cop in a suburb."

Her first shift on the street was rather quiet and she was glad that nothing happened this early in her career. Over the course of the first week, the two officers began to bond with Liza being critical, but fair. They sat down at the end of the week and reviewed the high and low points of Lissa's performance.

On her first night off, Lissa and Rob went to a movie and then out for a snack. Lissa was becoming more comfortable with Rob by the day. On her second night she just sat home and relaxed. She called Rob at his work and invited him to her house on her last night off for dinner. She told him that, if he wanted, he could bring an overnight bag, but made clear that there would be no sex. They had a quiet dinner and then watched television and cuddled. After watching the ten o'clock news, Lissa announced that she was going to bed. She and Rob walked into the bedroom and Lissa went into the bathroom, returning in pajamas. Rob entered the bathroom and walked out totally naked. He had an erection and said, "Nothing to worry about.

I cannot sleep with clothes, but nothing will happen, I promise." He slid into the bed and Lissa slid over to snuggle with him. She felt the smoothness of his bare skin and fell asleep with her head on his shoulder. When the alarm sounded at four-thirty a.m., Lissa felt awake and ready for whatever came. She went into the bathroom and showered. She walked out wearing only a towel around her wet hair. She saw Rob admiring her naked body and her shapely curves. Rob went in and showered. As he walked out of the bathroom, he saw Lissa wearing a sports bra and putting on a mesh tee shirt. Over the shirt she strapped in her bulletproof vest and then put on the uniform shirt for the day. She was still naked from the waist down and glanced to see Rob's reaction when she bent over to put on her panties and uniform pants. She went out to the living room closet to retrieve her Sam Browne gun belt and then went over to a table where the charger for her portable police radio was sitting. She and Rob walked out together and she gave him a passionate kiss saying, "We really will have to do this again, soon." ***

Liza was in the roll call room when Lissa walked in. They got their assignment and listened to the information that the Sergeant wanted to know. As they walked down the hallway to the parking lot Liza said, "I feel like being a passenger today, you drive." They drove to a White Castle Restaurant for their morning coffee and casually cruised the streets chatting. Liz asked,

"Do you have a special person in your life, Lissa?" Lissa smiled and said, "Actually, I think I do. He is a new attorney in the Kenton County Commonwealth Attorney's Office and a real gentleman. How about you?" Liza laughed and said, "I have been married twice. First to another cop who couldn't keep his dick in his pants and then to a paramedic who decided balling his female partner in their rig should not concern me. The non-public safety men I have dated seemed to have a real problem with dealing with a strong woman."

The police radio cracked out a call to the Kroger grocery store at 1412 Vine Street for security holding a shoplifter. Lissa stepped on the gas and they were there in three minutes. They walked into the security office where a black male was sitting in a chair handcuffed. The loss prevention officer said the suspect attempted to leave the store with six containers of baby formula. Liza asked the suspect to tell his side of the story and the man started crying, saying

"My infant child has no food and I have been laid off work for almost a month." Lissa looked at the security guy and said, "What is the total cost of the formula?" The officer answered, "$12.67." Lissa reached into her pocket and pulled out a twenty dollar bill saying, "Now he didn't steal anything. Take off the handcuffs." She looked at the guy and said, "You won't be so lucky next time, so find a different way."

The two cops got back into the cruiser and Liza demanded to know, "Why did you do that?" Lissa smiled and said, "Baby formula is not exactly marketable to buy drugs. The world is only a few paychecks from where that guy is." Liza said, "I am duly impressed."

There were just riding up and down the streets when Lissa asked, "Tell me about your last recruit. He sounds like he was a stand-up guy." Liza got a sad look on her face and said, "His name was Matt Davis and he came to Cincinnati from California. He had a lot of bad luck in his time here. He came to me after being forced to go to California when his father fell off a cruise ship and died. He was shot at on the two-week ride break in the Police Academy and was involved in a fatal shooting that resulted in a Federal indictment which he beat. He saved my ass in a shooting that I was involved in because he went back and found the gun that the suspect threw away. He left the PD and went to Law School and married another cop. She was pregnant with his baby when she was ambushed and killed in District Two. They couldn't save the baby and he just could not live with that. He drove to a park in District Three and shot himself in the head on a park bench overlooking the Ohio River. Just a sad story."

Liza looked at Lissa and said, "So what is your story?" Lissa said, "This is what I wanted to do since I was a child in Tennessee. I graduated college and the closest major city was Cincinnati. I moved to Newport and got a job working as a guard until I got raped at work. After the story made the news, I got an offer of a job with the Kentucky Attorney General's Sexual Assault Task Force and worked sex cases all over the State. A Cincinnati detective named

Robin Miller convinced me to get in the process for the

Police Department and the rest is history."

Liza asked, "How did being raped impact your relationships with men?" Lissa replied, "It had a major impact. I still can't let a man inside of me because of the revolting experience that I went through. The guy I am with now seems to understand and accept that, at least for now. I am getting more and more comfortable with him and hope that I will be able to have sex with him someday." Liza looked over at her driver and said simply, "Wow!"

The first four weeks of Lissa's training flew by. As she prepared to move on to her new FTO Liza said,

"Understand this. We all have different standards that we score by and you need to adapt to the rules that the FTO sets. All that you need to care about is getting through this process so that you can get out on your own and play by your own rules. The first week that you are back with me, we will get back into my rules. You are going to make a good cop, so don't let anyone screw that up. See you in eight weeks."

***

Douglas Daily had twenty-one years on the job and had been an FTO for almost ten of them. He introduced himself to Lissa and said, "All I expect from you is perfection. Anything short of that results in flogging, beatings and persecution." As he said it, Lissa could see the big smile on his face. He looked at her and said, "All I care about is that we keep each other safe and go out and do the best job we can. Midnights takes some getting adjusted to, so I am in no hurry to evaluate your every move." Daily looked at her FTO book and said, "I love following Officer Seemoan. She potty trains the recruits well."

Lissa had never really seen the City when it closes down. Dailey told that between four and five-thirty in the morning the only people out were the paper delivery people and a few people who go to work early. The drunks were already in jail or had made it home and the burglars were snuggled in their bed with their work already done.

They were lazily patrolling the streets when they got a fight run outside of a bar on John Street in the West End. As they were pulling up to the scene, Lissa saw a guy retrieve a tire iron from the trunk of a car and start moving toward another man in front of the bar. The cruiser had not yet come to a complete stop when Lissa bailed out the passenger door hitting the drunk waist high with her shoulder. Two other cops later told her she had a career as a safety in the NFL in her future. When they got

123

the suspect cuffed up, Lissa retrieved the guy's driver's license and called for a warrant check. The dispatcher came back with, "Signal 30F" which means the guy had a felony warrant. Daily jumped on the radio asking, "What is the F?" The dispatcher replied, "Subject is wanted for Aggravated Murder. I am confirming the warrant at this moment.   The warrant is confirmed. You are to transport the subject to the Homicide Unit immediately."

After they dropped the suspect off at CIS, Daily looked at Lissa and said, "What the hell were you thinking?" Lissa did not hesitate as she said, "I knew the guy had his back to me and I knew that I could hit him before he could react." Daily replied, "Lady, if you want to end up on the Law Enforcement Memorial Wall in Washington, do it with someone else in the car. I can't fault the outcome, but make sure you tell your partner what you are going to do. I am not old enough to die of a heart attack. I do like the fact that you had a rational explanation for why you did what you did." The rest of the night passed without incident.

Daily let Lissa drive the second night. She saw an older model car pull out of a convenience store parking lot without turning on its headlights. Daily told her to wait until they reached an illuminated area prior to lighting the driver up so they would be able to see inside the car. Lissa approached the driver and ordered him to turn off the engine. When he refused, Lissa reached inside the car to grab the keys, at which point the driver jammed the gas pedal dragging Lissa as her arm got caught in the steering wheel. The car slammed into a parked van and the driver put the car in reverse. Daily, standing to the rear of the car, drew his gun and fired seven shots into the rear window, hitting the driver with two of them. Lissa got her arm loose from the entanglement and screamed "OFFICER NEEDS ASSISTANCE" into her radio. The driver was slumped over the wheel with car still in gear and Lissa fought to get the car into Park.

The sounds of sirens coming from all directions created a surreal environment and the area was flooded with blue and red within minutes. Daily was livid and said, "Don't ever reach inside a car. We had a cop killed doing that. Homicide and a supervisor will be here shortly, so be prepared to tell your story over and over." The driver of the car was still alive, but barely. The paramedic unit quickly threw him onto a gurney and transported him to the hospital with a police unit following behind.

Lissa was taken to CIS to be interviewed by the Homicide detectives. She told them, "I made a mistake reaching into the car to grab the keys and all my partner was doing was protecting me. It is my fault that my partner had to shoot."

When she finally got back home, there was a message from Liza to call her immediately. Liza wanted to make sure that she was okay and what had happened. After Lissa explained all of the events Liza said, "You were lucky that you had a good partner. Did you learn a lesson?"

***

Lissa needed her three days off to get her head unscrambled. She and Rob decided to go to the Horseshoe Casino for an evening of gambling and drinks. He drove to her house and they took a cab to the Casino, which is just outside of the downtown area. They took a cab back to her house and she said, "Do you want to stay the night?" Rob said, "I would like that."

When Rob came out of the bathroom naked Lissa was already under the covers. He slid into the bed and she snuggled right up to him. It only took seconds to decide that she was naked as well. She looked into his eyes and said, "I think I am ready. Move slowly and be prepared to stop." He looked at her and said, "I understand." She liked his hands roaming softly all over her body and was feeling a wetness that she had never felt before. She felt his erection throbbing in excitement of what might come. Rob looked her in the eyes and said, "Climb on top, that way you will be in control of what happens." Lissa rolled over to the other side of the bed and opened the drawer on the nightstand. She pulled out a package containing a condom and rolled back over to his side of the bed. She ripped open the package and slowly unwound it on his erect penis. She then straddled him and directed his manhood inside of her wetness. She looked down at his face and could see that he was enjoying every second. As she moved up and down, she could feel something special going on inside her. The feeling that she was experiencing was something she had never known before. When she reached her first ever climax, she was pounding up and down on him and heard him gasp and shoot his load. The pulsating that she now felt inside her was a good feeling. She collapsed onto Rob and felt the erection slowly dissolving inside her.

***

Her Phase Three FTO was a ten-year veteran named Dontonio Murray. They got into the cruiser and he demanded her FTO book. As he reviewed the entries he said, "You are very lucky that you drew two good cops. Recruits who get this far usually make it to the end. Do what you are told and you will have no problem with me." It was a cold evening in Cincinnati and Murray asked, "Why is your window down?" Lissa said, "I was told to always keep it down so that I can hear the sounds of the City. With it up, I might miss a scream for help or a gunshot." Murray thought for a second and said, "I like that, good answer."

Lissa had finally reached the last stage of the field training process. She and Liza reviewed the evaluations of the other two training officers before they left the District for their first shift. Liza told Lissa, "You have shown definite improvement in each of the stages and that is a good thing. The area we need to work on is that you react too quickly to things happening, but that will come as you mature as a cop. This job is not about catching the bad guys at all cost. It is about going home at the end of the shift to be able to catch more bad guys tomorrow. After this four weeks you will be transferred to another District. That is the policy. I make it a rule not to socialize with any of my recruits, but once you are out of the training, you are my peer and I would love to be your friend. These last four weeks are going to be a breeze. We will just go out and do our job and try to stay out of trouble."

Her final week in the FTO program brought a note that she was being transferred to District Two, which was less than two miles from her house.

CHAPTER ELEVEN

Lissa and Rob's relationship continued to grow. Rob took her to his parents' house for dinner and they planned a trip to Tennessee for him to meet her folks. They discussed moving in together, but there was a major problem with that.

Cincinnati has a residency requirement and so did the Commonwealth Attorney. Rob discussed taking the Ohio Bar Examination so that he could practice in Ohio and they decided that the relationship was working well in its current form.

Lissa reported to District Two for her first shift as a police officer. She would be working the power shift from eight o'clock at night until four in the morning. It is called power shift because that is the time frame that most crimes are committed. Up until this, she had been a probationary police officer. There were two other females on her shift and she was not treated warmly by anyone at the District. She decided that she needed to prove her worth to be accepted and took it all in stride.

She was assigned to work Car 2402 and her house was in her beat. It was a two-person car so she would be able to learn the streets in the District. Her partner was a male with five years on the job. The first thing he told her was, "I would really rather work alone, that way the only one I have to protect is me." Lissa replied, "All you need to do is teach me the streets and I will request to be moved to a one person car, okay?" He said, "District Two is the quietest District in the City. Write a ticket per shift and the bosses don't care what you do with the rest of your time. The only exception to that is any call around shift change at ten o'clock they expect you to jump on so they don't have to pull a car out of roll call to handle. Doesn't matter where in the District the call is, got it?"

Her partner was right. They only handled three calls in the eight-hour shift, but wrote one ticket for running a red light.

Her next shift was partnered with one of the females who had eight years of experience. They were assigned to the farthest eastern point where the City line meets the County. The female told her that there were several neighboring agencies who were always willing to come and help and introduced her to cops from Madeira, Fairfax and Mariemont PDs.

Lissa decided she liked the four ten-hour shifts much better than the five eight-hour shifts. She found she really enjoyed her days off to spend time with Rob.

Lisa was on her first night working alone when she got a call for a purse snatching on Madison Road. As she approached the intersection, she saw a male running with a purse in his hand. She jumped out of the cruiser and gave chase, running almost two blocks before the suspect ducked into an alcove. Remembering what Liza had told her about catching the bad guy at all costs, she called for help and took cover behind a parked car. After a couple of minutes of silence, she saw the muzzle flash of two gunshots and heard the bullets hit the car she was behind. Yelling into the radio, "SHOTS FIRED, SHOTS FIRED," she heard the All County Broadcast tones and the dispatcher say, "Cincinnati officer needs assistance, Whetzel and Madison. Officer reports shots being fired. Any available unit in the area respond." Four cars arrived in less than two minutes and not one of them matched in color. One was from the Village of Fairfax, one from the Sheriff's Department, one from the City of Madeira and one from the Village of Mariemont. In the background there was the sounds of sirens coming from all directions. Lissa yelled from behind the car, "Pal, we have you outnumbered. Unless this is the night you intend to die, throw out the gun and walk out with your hands where we can see them." As more and more police units came screaming to a stop, the moron decided that this would not end well and walked out of the alcove with his hands in the air. He was immediately tackled by two big cops and handcuffed. Lissa was going to get to go home tonight.   ***

Because she had joined the department under the lateral entry program, she had accrued vacation time of a twoyear veteran. She and Rob left to drive to Tennessee for a getaway. They decided to check into a hotel rather than stay at her parents so her parents would not have to see them sleeping together. They spent one day in Lafollette and then drove south to Knoxville to relax and enjoy each other's company. They walked the downtown area and held hands like two young lovebirds. They talked about the possibility of getting married, but their jobs made that extremely difficult. The fact that they both loved their current jobs complicated the situation even further.

**

When Lissa returned to work, she found that she was being transferred back to District One. She was happy to leave District Two because she just did not fit in with the other cops assigned there. She would also be back on a ten-hour schedule working ten at night until eight in the morning. She also knew that she would cross paths with Liza for two hours on the days when they both were working.

Lissa and Rob decided that she would leave clothes at his condo and spend her off days there. He could come to her place on other days. They talked about the possibility of having children, but Lissa said she just wasn't ready for that.

She enjoyed the fact that she would be working alone. In a two-person car two factors exist that create issues. One is that there seems to be a need to impress the other officer with machismo and the second is a feeling of need to protect your partner at all costs. Working alone makes safety paramount and the likelihood of making a mistake diminishes appreciably.

Lissa answered all of her radio calls and tried to be as proactive as she could be. She didn't volunteer for overtime, but took it as necessary. She wanted to be a quiet and unseen figure, just another cop.

Lissa looked at the bulletin board and saw the posting of the officers eligible to take the Sergeant's test. She was surprised to see her name on the list, but then remembered that all of her lateral entry status brought with it all of her law enforcement time and the time she was in the academy. She thought long and hard about signing up, but decided she still had too much to learn and chose not to.

It was four a.m. and the streets of District One were empty and peaceful. She was driving slowly north on Central Parkway and had just passed the District when she saw a male standing in the center of the four lane road. She stopped the cruiser and asked the black male in his fifties if he needed help. The male walked over the cruiser, pulled

a revolver from his coat pocket and pointed it at Lissa. He punched her in the face and ordered her into the passenger seat of the cruiser. Lissa had to climb over the console and the in-car computer to get to the passenger side and, when she did, the male subject jumped into the driver's seat and roared northbound on Central Parkway. In fear for her life, Lissa drew her semi-auto and fired two shots into the subject's head. Pathologists would later report that both shots actually went into the same hole.

The cruiser careened to the left and struck a building that formerly housed a Cincinnati brewery. Lissa punched the panic button on her radio and screamed, "Central Parkway, North of the District, Officer Needs Assistance, Shots fired."   The response she got was immediate. Cops in the District ran out to their cars and were there in seconds. When the first officers arrived, Lissa was holding her hand over her swollen left eye and paramedics were called. She sat frozen in the car clutching her .40 caliber handgun as the suspect sat slumped over the wheel of the police car.

The Communications Section called the Police Chief who arrived at the scene within twenty minutes. Cops were all asking what the hell had happened, but Lissa was dazed and just stared off into space. The Chief ordered her taken to University of Cincinnati Medical Center by the paramedics. When the Coroner removed the body of the suspect, officers recovered a .38 caliber silver handgun from the driver's seat. The suspect had no identification on him, but one of the veteran cops recognized him as a homeless man who wandered Central Parkway late at night and believed that his name was Dennis Flagg. A criminal record check showed Flagg has one hundred twenty-seven arrests for misdemeanor beefs such as trespassing and disorderly conduct, but no history of violence. Rumors ran rampant that this was a case of 'Suicide by Cop,' but no one would ever know his motivation.

When Lissa woke at the hospital, she saw Liza and Robin in her room. They told her that her parents were on the way from Tennessee and that a man, claiming to be her boyfriend, was waiting in the lobby. Liza went out and got Rob who bent over the hospital bed to gently give Liza a hug. He said that he had heard about what happened on the radio as he was driving to work and had been at the hospital for hours. He told Lissa, "You wouldn't believe the number of cops out there. I saw the Police Chief, Captains, Lieutenants, Sergeants and regular cops milling around to make sure you are okay. Lissa's left eye was bandaged, but the doctor assured her she would be fine in a few days. He told Rob that she would be released and that he could take her home in a few hours. Rob left to get coffee from the cafeteria and a delivery kid brought in a flower arrangement. Lissa asked Robin to read the card and

Robin said, "From the staff of the Kentucky Attorney General, we are glad you are safe." Sgt. Harrison from the FOP stuck her head in the room door and asked, "Do you need anything Mellissa?" Lissa smiled and said, "No thanks, my friends are taking real good care of me."

Rob drove Lissa home in silence. When she was on the couch, Rob sat down and said, "You scared the hell outta me. I forgot how dangerous your job really is. I am not sure I can handle the stress of not knowing if you are going to make it home. But we can talk about it later. Go to sleep now." When she woke from a sound sleep, there were messages on her phone. One was from the Police Chief saying he was glad she was safe and one from the Internal Investigation Section saying they needed to interview her as soon as she felt able.

Liza stopped by the house to check on Lissa and said, "I have been involved in a deadly force case. You will be on paid administrative leave until the department shrink clears you to go back. That won't happen until you have healed from the injuries. The rat squad from Internal will want to interview you as well. They are not your friends, so be careful. You have the right to have an FOP rep or a lawyer with you when you talk to them. In my shooting, they treated me like shit, like I was the criminal."

Rob came over after he was done with work and brought take-out Chinese for them to share.   He asked her what had happened and her reply was simply, "I don't know, I honestly don't remember. It is all just a blur to me."

Lissa was told that it would be a minimum of two weeks before the doctor would clear her to return to work. He sent the police department a note that said, "Patient is not to be contacted until cleared by me.   Her physical injuries will only be complicated by additional stress."

Investigators determined the gun Flagg was carrying had been reported stolen from a vehicle less than a month before the incident. They interviewed countless homeless people to try to figure out what caused the man to snap, but no one could shed any light on his mental state.   When they were finally able to interview Lissa at her home, she told them, "I can't be of much help. I honestly don't recall anything about the incident." The Chief investigator, Lt. Carl Saunders, looked at Lissa and said, "There is no doubt that this is a good shoot. We found the gun he had and it has his prints on the gun and the bullets. We don't know why he attacked you, but once the doctors clear you, you are authorized to return to duty." Lissa was relieved and the investigators left.

Lissa made the appointment to see the psychologist and was happy it was the same one as her pre-employment.

Dr. Don asked her, "What do you remember about the incident, Melissa?" Melissa replied, "Absolutely nothing. I don't even remember working that night." "Are you feeling any remorse that you took a life, Melissa?" Lissa said, "I have no feelings about it all because all I know about it is what I have been told. The investigators told me that they had no doubt it was a good shoot, but not having any personal recollection of it makes it impossible for me to feel anything about it. I feel bad that I am not feeling anything about killing a human being." The doc said she could return to duty, but that he would recommend to the department Lissa be put on light duty for a few weeks. That meant the desk or the Telephone Crime Reporting Unit, which would not be as stressful as the street.

***

Her relationship with Rob was starting to deteriorate. He told her that he didn't believe that he could continue a relationship with a person whose life was on the line every time she went to work. Lissa was beginning to understand what male cops wives felt when their husbands put on the monkey suit to go to work. They were sitting in her living room watching television when she asked, "You really do want children, don't you Rob?" Rob replied, "Yes, I really do." Lissa continued, "I had a child and don't believe that I want any more. Maybe it's time we think about moving in different directions. You have been the best thing that has happened in my life so far, but I do not think that this can work long term. If it is going to end, I want it to be on good terms." It was decided that they would both move on in different directions, but try to remain friends.

***

Lissa was assigned to TCRU which works eight a.m. to four p.m. taking non-violent crime reports over the telephone. She quickly learned the cops assigned to TCRU were there because they had been stripped of their police powers pending disciplinary action or had pissed off a boss.

She actually enjoyed the mundane duties of talking on the phone with people who had their lawn mowers or bicycles

138

stolen from their garage. It was low stress and that, for whatever reason, was what she needed right now.

Lissa used her time at TCRU to see what opportunities might be available at the department. She saw that applications were being accepted for the Canine Unit. Since she was an animal lover, she put in for it.

At the interview, Lissa was told that the shifts for canine officers was noon until eight and eight until four in the morning. The position had a take-home car and the canine officers were on call at other times. She would get a dog and then go through twelve weeks of training to get the dog certified as a 'working dog' by the State of Ohio. She told the Unit Commander that she would enjoy the opportunity. She received notification two weeks later that she was being transferred to the Special Operations Unit and that she was to report to meet her new 'partner' the following Monday.

Lissa was introduced to Sheba, an eighteen-month-old female pure bred German Shepard. The dog had been brought from Germany and she was told that her commands would be given in German so that only she would be able to communicate with the dog.

The training for the dog and the handler was intense and involved the dog not reacting to explosions or gunfire. Lissa developed a total respect for the guys who dressed up in padded suits and then were bitten or knocked on their ass by a large dog at a full run. The dog had to complete a grueling obstacle course, much tougher than the one she took applying for the police department.

At the graduation ceremony, she was assigned a marked car which she would take home every night. She would be working the night shift and would report to District One for briefing. She would then work citywide to cover any requests for the dog. The dog was cross-trained to search for and identify drugs and would be called for when search warrants would be executed.

She would be compensated for the food and veterinary care for the dog, but any toys or other things she wanted would be at her expense. Lissa bought the dog a bed and placed it at the foot of her own bed and the dog and handler developed a fast and firm bond. Lissa would take Sheba out into the backyard and they would play like a couple of kids. Sheba seemed to love yellow tennis balls and Lissa would give her one every time she did something good.

Lissa had Court for a traffic ticket she had written so she left Sheba at the house. She was driving back to the house when a call came out over the radio to her address to investigate a male screaming for help. Lissa jumped on the radio announcing, "Advise District Two units responding that the Linwood Avenue address is my residence and that my canine is in the house. I am responding from the downtown area and will arrive in seven to eight minutes." When she pulled up in front of her house, two marked police cars were parked on the street. The three cops walked up to the front door and Lissa unlocked it. They entered the house to see Sheba laying on the floor growling and a scared skinny teenager frozen to a wall in fear. Lissa called Sheba back away from the kid and the two cops handcuffed him. Lissa walked to the back entrance, which had been forced open, and returned saying, "You are just having a bad day, huh, moron?" The nineteen-year-old, who had already wet his pants, looked at the cops and said, "Just take me to jail. Keep that fucking dog away from me." One of the cops looked at Lissa and said, "Damn, I love easy and it don't get any easier than this."

***

Now that Lissa and Rob had parted ways, she began going out with Robin and Liza. They would go to different events and bars and laugh when the wannabe studs would hit on them. Since all three were pretty and fit, they rarely bought their own drinks. They would tolerate the flirting of the guys until they tired and one of them would let the guy see the gun under the jacket. That usually scared them off. Lissa came to find out that, with Sheba there, she really didn't need a man in her life. Sheba just loved unconditionally.

***

Lissa had just completed a call from the University of Cincinnati Police to search a car for drugs. When Sheba failed to hit on

141

anything in or around the vehicle, Lissa smiled and said, "Sorry bout your luck, maybe next time." She put Sheba back in the car just as the radio broadcast a fight run at a bar three blocks away. Lissa pulled up in front of the Toke Me Bar and Grille and walked in the front door where she encountered a man at least six feet five inches and probably near three hundred pounds. The guy saw that she was alone and said, "Lady, you are screwed." Reaching down to her belt, she hit the release button for the back door of the cruiser and yelled, "SHEBA!" It wasn't ten seconds and the ninety pound dog was sitting at her right side offering a guttural growl and bared all of her teeth. The man took one look at the dog and said, "Maybe it's me that's screwed."

She loved that she only made radio runs that interested her and to specific requests for searching for drugs, suspects and lost kids. She and Sheba would play in the City parks at two in the morning while the rest of the world slept.

Lissa received a request from the North College Hill Police to respond for a search. They had just had an armed robbery at a McDonalds Restaurant and had the suspect pinned in a wooded area. When she pulled up, there were marked cars and cops with shotguns and tactical rifles covering all of the corners of the wooded area. With Sheba attached to a twelve-foot leash, Lissa yelled, "YO MORON, come out with your hands where we can see them." When that generated no response, Lissa said, "Speak Sheba." The dog barked wildly for a moment and

Lissa yelled, "See, I am not kidding. The question you need to answer is whether you want to stop at the hospital before they take your sorry ass off to jail." Looking at two cops standing close by, Lissa announced, "Oh well, I tried." The two went trekking into the woods to flush out the suspect. The twenty-three-year-old junkie was hiding in a bush when he saw the cop and the dog approaching with a flashlight. He decided he could outrun the dog and took off at a sprint.

Lissa hit the button that allowed the dog off the leash and Sheba was on the young punk within seconds. The dog went airborne and hit the kid in the left shoulder with all of her ninety pounds of force. When they both hit the ground, Sheba was back up and on top of the strungout kid drooling on his face while she growled at him. Lissa called the dog off and called for cops to come in and cuff this piece of trash. As she had warned, Sheba had separated the kid's shoulder with the impact, so they had to take him to the hospital. Because there was no bite involved, Lissa was not required to complete the mound of paperwork that a bite requires.

***

The two were playing with a tennis ball in a park when a burglar alarm at a warehouse nearby came out on the radio. Lissa looked at Sheba and said, "Let's go to work" and the dog ran to the back door for her to open it. When they arrived one of the uniforms said, "The back door has been kicked in." Lissa opened the back door and put the leash on Sheba and three cops and the dog walked in the rear entrance. They were walking along the large warehouse when one of the cops pointed upward to a row of boxes where a man could be seen laying. Lissa stopped and the dog immediately sat down next to her. She yelled, "Come down or I send the dog up to help you down." The man yelled back, "Go ahead, and send the dog up here."

Lissa unleashed the dog who cocked her head to the right and then took off running around the boxes. Moments later she returned, sat down next to her handler. She cocked her head to the left and took off running around the left side of the boxes, returning moments later and taking her place next to Lissa. A few seconds passed and the dog took off at a dead run. Moments later a scream was heard and the man fell fifteen feet to the cement floor, having been bitten in the ass by the dog. Lissa walked over to the moaning man, looked down and said, "Moron."

Lisa and Sheba had been together for almost a year. They were at a canine training session at the Firearm Training facility just north of the City when the supervisor walked over and asked her if she would like to take Sheba and compete in the United States Police Canine Association national competition in Jacksonville, Florida. Lissa said, "We would be honored to represent Cincinnati, sir."

There were handlers and dogs of all breeds from all over the country represented. The participants were told they would be tested on tracking, search, dealing with aggressive suspects and drug searches and scored on their success. Being one of sixty teams of what was probably the best canines in the country was a bit intimidating, but Sheba did not appear to be concerned at all.

The first test was a search for a wanted person. She found a jacket that has been tossed, then a shirt, then a pair of pants. She tracked for over a mile through a creek bed. Lissa was dripping wet when they encountered the suspect, who was hiding in a tree. Sheba jumped up and tried to bite the trainer, but he was just a foot or two too high for the dog to make the leap.

Lissa looked up at the man and said, "You don't know this dog, pal. She will find a way and then bite you till you fall." Sheba backed up about ten yards and then ran and leaped, missing a bite by only inches. When the dog moved back another five yards, the trainer yell, "Call the dog off lady. I am coming down." Lissa reached into her pocket and pulled out a yellow tennis ball and Sheba put in her mouth shaking the ball vigorously because she knew she had done well.

Sheba recovered three baggies of drugs from different parts of a car, but lost points for missing two more. Lissa said, "It was not the dog's fault, it was mine."

The two finished sixth in the competition, the highest that any team from Cincinnati had finished in the last twelve years. She got an 'attaboy' from the supervisor when they returned.

CHAPTER TWELVE

Lissa had been back to work about a week when she found an envelope in her bin at District One. The envelope contained an application form to attend a training hosted by Alcohol, Tobacco and Firearms for explosive ordinance detection dog. The form said the training would consist of six ten-hour days, then one day off, followed by six more ten-hour days. "It will held at the Federal Law Enforcement Training Center in Glynco, Georgia and the final examination would require the canine to locate seven different devices." If the dog and handler missed any one of the seven, they would fail the certification test. Lissa was given the choice of driving to Georgia in her canine cruiser or flying there with the dog. She chose to drive so that Sheba would not have to ride in the belly of the plane.

The two left Cincinnati and drove south on I-75. She stopped every two hours at a rest stop so that Sheba could stretch and do her business. They drove all the way to Memphis, Tennessee before stopping for the night. Lissa brought food, a water bowl and toys for Sheba, but needed to go out and pick up dinner for herself. When she pulled back into the Hampton Suites parking lot, she was surprised to see four marked Memphis Police cars at the front entrance.

When she reached her floor, she saw four male cops standing outside her room door and heard a male voice screaming, "Someone call the Police!" Lissa approached the room door with her badge and ID card in hand and asked what the problem was. One of the cops looked at her credentials and starting laughing. He said whoever was in the room was screaming that there was a killer dog in the room.

Lissa used her room key to enter the room and the five cops walked in. They found a frail man standing on a table and Sheba giving out a guttural growl. Lissa called the dog who slowly walked over and sat at Lissa's side. The man came down from the table and the cops asked what he was doing. The man replied, "I am the night manager of the hotel. We received a call that someone had brought an animal into the hotel. I knocked on the door and, when no one answered, used my all access key to open the door. I walked into the room and this beast came out of the bathroom growling at me. I jumped on the table in fear for my life.

All the cops were laughing as the front of the manager's pants which were very wet. Lissa said, "Sir, didn't you take the time to see who the room was rented to? I am a
Cincinnati, Ohio Police officer on my way to training in
Georgia. I listed on the check-in form that I was a
Cincinnati Police Canine Officer and that there would be two in the room. I do hope you brought a second pair of pants!"

The four cops wished Lissa well and laughed when Sheba glared at the manager and snarled as he left the room which now smelled like urine. Lissa yelled out into the hall, "Any chance of getting someone in here to clean the smell in this room? The

Memphis cops were now doubled over in laughter as the little man's face flushed a deep red color.

Just like at home, Sheba made herself comfortable at the foot of the king-size bed and the two slept well. Lissa fed Sheba before they left the room and then put her in the cruiser to get her complimentary breakfast from the hotel. They got back onto the Interstate and continued through Atlanta and finally reached the FLETC training center.

When she pulled up to the Security gate, the uniformed officer demanded her badge and identification. Lissa looked startled and said, "A marked police vehicle doesn't constitute ID?"

The officer glared back and replied, "Lady, you do what you are told to do at work and so do I." Lissa looked sheepishly at the guy and said, "You are absolutely right and I apologize." She produced her police ID and badge and handed them to the officer, who was now smiling.

The officer gave her the directions to the main building where she would register and get her accommodation assignment.

The receptionist at the front desk was in her early twenties with a smile that would illuminate a small city. She logged Lissa in and then asked, "Do you want to put the dog in our kennel or stay in the room with you?" With a glance intended to cause serious bodily harm Lissa answered, "This dog and I don't part company!" The receptionist never lost her smile as she handed Lissa the room key and a map with directions to the housing area.

Lissa and Sheba arrived at the classroom about ten minutes early. There were nine other handlers and their canine partners in the room. She started looking at the patches on the uniforms and saw Santa Rosa, California, Las Vegas Metro, Boston, Wichita, Kansas, Roswell, New Mexico, Tampa, Florida, Birmingham, Alabama, Portland, Maine, and New Orleans, Louisiana. The instructor walked into the room and took them to an area where there were Danish, muffins and doggie treats.

While they stood and ate, he told them that they had never experienced training like they would receive in the next two weeks. He told the group that they would be learning from twelve o'clock noon until ten o'clock p.m. every day and that there was no excused time for any reason. He also told them that, based on previous classes, it was likely that only four of the ten would leave with a certified dog.

The instructor took them out to the parking lot and told them to follow him in their cruisers. He took them to a remote field where there were two other instructors waiting. He had the handlers stand in a line spaced with room for the dogs and told them to order the canines to lay down. Lissa gave the command in German and Sheba laid down immediately. The handlers stood waiting for the next command when they heard a deafening explosion less than fifty feet from where they stood. The dog from Santa Rosa PD jumped up from its position and the instructor told the handler, "Thanks for coming all the way to Georgia, your dog just failed the first test. Have a safe career."

Everyone in the class looked shocked and the cop next to Lissa said simply, "HOLY SHIT!" The instructor looked at the remaining nine handlers and said, "We are not here to be bad asses, but a dog that jumps is a threat when searching for explosives and we need to weed them out quickly. This is only the beginning; it gets much more difficult from here."

The first day was spent teaching the dogs the smells of military grade and homemade explosives. By the end of the day, both Lissa and Sheba were beat up and worn out. Lissa thought to herself, "This is gonna be a bitch!"

The instructors worked with each handler and dog individually to train them how to react to a 'hit'. When the dog was successful, they were given a few minutes of playtime to show gratitude. The dogs were trained to lay down and remain motionless when they uncovered an explosive. At the end of day two, the dogs were required to identify the case (there were five) containing C4 military grade explosives. The canine from Tampa was sent home after the test.

By the end of the sixth day Lissa and Sheba needed a day to unwind. Lissa took Sheba out to a field and played with her tennis ball and a frisbie. Sheba would go airborne to snatch the frisbie out of the sky and run back. She would then sit in front of Lissa and wait for her to remove it from her mouth and then immediately turn around for the next throw. After an hour or so, Sheba's tongue was hanging out and she was breathing hard, but showed no sign of wanting to quit. Lissa had brought bottled water for both she and the dog to drink and they walked the campus for almost an hour getting their breath back.

When they returned on Monday, they were notified that the handler and canine from Roswell had decided not to continue. Lissa thought, "Three down and we are just starting the second week." The first thing the remaining students saw was a car obliterated by an explosion. The instructor looked at the class and said, "Had you been within five hundred feet when that blew, you and your dog would have received a hero's funeral service."

There were seven left when it got the final day and the final test. The teams were separated and taken to seven different locations. Lissa and Sheba were taken to a parking lot and told to locate the explosive device where there were at least fifty cars parked. Lissa walked Sheba around each car in the lot, giving encouragement to the dog to find the bomb. When they arrived at a 2004 Ford Escort Sheba sniffed around the rear bumper and laid down motionless.

Lissa called out, "I have a hit!" The instructor walked over and reached under the bumper, pulling out a pipe bomb. He said, "Congratulate your dog. It just passed the test." Lissa ordered the dog up and reached into her pocket for a new tennis ball, taunting the dog who was now yapping and jumping around. Lissa tossed the ball and Sheba caught it on the first bounce.

The second location was an outdoor stadium. They were given no instructions other than find the device. Lissa thought to herself, "Where the hell am I supposed to start?" Lissa took the dog to every area that she could not see clearly. They saw a couple of packages in the stands, but Sheba walked right by them. When they completed the search of the stands, Lissa took Sheba into the restrooms and tunnels, but they found nothing. Lissa began a grid search of the outer concourse when Sheba dropped in front of a trash receptacle. Lissa yelled out, "I've got a hit!" and the instructor walked over and removed a package of dynamite and a timer. The instructor repeated, "Congratulate your dog. It just passed the second test. Only five more to go!" It was lunch time and they were given a break. Lissa thought to herself, "Sheba is doing her job perfectly. I am the one that is not going to survive this stress!"

Sheba found the devices at the third, fourth and fifth locations and the team was given their dinner break. The sixth location was a housing unit and they had to do a room by room search that took almost two hours. She identified the device and Lissa hugged the dog knowing that there only one location left.

They arrived at the seventh location. It was filled with people and Lissa thought, "What the hell are we looking for?" Sheba walked around the room which had more than fifty people in it. Lissa pulled her to check under tables and chairs until Sheba pulled her leash dragging Lissa across the room. Sheba walked up to a male standing in a corner and dropped to the floor. Lissa was trying to interpret what Sheba was reacting to, but saw that the dog's eyes were glued on the male. Lissa yelled out, "I think I need help here, which caused the man to break out in laughter. Watching Sheba intently, the man slowly opened his coat to show a suicide vest and yelled out, "Give our newest certified team a round of applause", to which the whole room started clapping. Meanwhile, Sheba's gaze never left the man until she was called off by Lissa. Lissa asked the guy, "Aren't you a little afraid that the dog is going to think I am in danger and attack?" The man laughed and said, "Lady, I have been bitten by the best police dogs this country has to offer."

Lissa collapsed onto the bed at the housing unit, totally drained. She was told that only three of the teams left were able to pass the training. Lissa cupped her hands on Sheba's face and yelled, "Damn, you are GOOD!"

CHAPTER THIRTEEN

The City had given Lissa four days off upon her return from the training. She rented an SUV and reserved a log cabin overlooking Cumberland Lake, about two and one-half hours south of Cincinnati.

The two spent the days playing and swimming in the ice cold water of the lake. Sheba was playing in the water and Lissa was lying in the grass watching as two uniformed
Kentucky Conservation officers approached. Lissa saw Sheba come out of the water at a dead run toward the two strange men and had to call her off. The dog came over to Lissa and sat perfectly straight, poised to protect her master. The officers looked at the dog and Lissa and told her that it is illegal in Kentucky to have a dog off a leash. Lissa carefully reached into her purse and the two officers immediately saw her .40 caliber handgun. Jumping back, the two cops reached for their guns. Sheba looked like she was ready to kill when Lissa yelled, "I am a Cincinnati cop. I am reaching for my badge and this is a working Cincinnati Police canine!" She slowly removed her hand from her purse and showed the two men her badge case with her ID and badge. The two young cops relaxed and asked what the two were doing. Lissa explained that they had just completed an intense training school at the Federal Law Enforcement Training

Center and were there to wind down and relax. She apologized for not having brought Sheba's leash and that they would leave immediately. During the entire conversation Sheba remained coiled and ready to strike. The Conservation cops looked at each other and said that they would not be returning to the area until after dark and that the dog needed to be on a leash or not there when they returned. Knowing that dark was several hours away, Lissa smiled and said simply, "Thank you. I appreciate the heads-up."

In the evenings inside the cabin, Sheba would lay close to the roaring fire while Lissa watched television or read. By the end of the fourth day, both Lissa and Sheba had relaxed and were ready to get back to work. Work was mundane after the intensity of the explosives training. The two rode around and caught bad guys and played in the parks in the wee hours of the morning.

Lissa found an envelope in her bin at the District. It ordered her to be at the PIG Marathon at six o'clock in the morning. The PIG Marathon is a twenty-six mile race that also serves as a qualifier for the historic Boston Marathon.

Lissa arrived at the police staging area and was told by an Assistant Police Chief that she would be walking the first mile of the race with her canine, assuring that there were no explosive devices on the route. She would then walk back on the other side of the street making the same check.

Lissa brought out a six-foot lead for Sheba and the two started the trek from the starting line east. They stopped at every package, trash receptacle and bench for Sheba to check. They had traveled about half the distance outbound when Sheba tugged on the leash and moved toward a bush just off the sidewalk. Sheba immediately laid down and went motionless. Lissa backed away to a safe distance and called Police Communications to have the bomb squad meet her. She left Sheba in her place as police cars, fire vehicles and the bomb truck arrived. She explained to the two bomb technicians that the dog had alerted to the bush next to where she was lying.

The bomb techs looked less than thrilled as they suited up with one hundred fifty pounds of gear. They had no belief that they were going to find anything, but had to follow protocol. As they approached the bush, Lissa called Sheba back to her side and the crowd of cops, spectators and news media gathered to watch the action.

The first tech pushed back the bush while the other looked into it. His right hand went up in the air and the two slowly backed away. Once safely away, the tech took off the helmet and told the police and fire supervisors that a stainless steel pressure cooker was in the bush. The police supervisors ordered the area cleared of the spectators and the fire commander called for the bomb robot. It took twenty minutes for the robot to be brought to the scene. It was operated by remote control and was able to x-ray the inside of the container. The X-ray was dark leading the operator to opine that it had a thin lead coating to stop the ability to x-ray. The operator was able to remotely get the robot to pick up the pressure cooker and take it to an open area. The bomb techs suited up again. This time without the attitude and approached the device to photograph it. Afraid to open it in case there was some form of tamper safeguard, they took their pictures and returned to where everyone was gathered. A police supervisor asked if it would be possible to throw fingerprint powder on the device and lift any prints. When the techs said yes, he ordered for the crime scene van which carries the powder and tape to lift prints. The techs came back with several good fingerprints for later analysis. The robot then picked up the container and took it to a large barrel which had been attached to a fire truck. The barrel was lead and designed to withstand a strong blast. The fire commander told the Assistant Police Chief that the device needed to be detonated because of the potential risk to all.

The techs placed the device inside the barrel and secured the top. They backed away and the bomb was remotely detonated. The barrel absorbed the blast, but the shock waves could be felt from five hundred feet away.

After watching the detonation, Lissa and Sheba walked across the street and began heading back toward the starting line. Sheba suddenly froze and laid down and there was now terror in Lissa's eyes. She screamed, "Bomb Techs, I need you NOW!" There was no hesitation this time as the two techs suited up and moved as quickly as their heavy gear would let them. They immediately located a second container in a trash receptacle just off the roadway. It was now time for the race to start and the Police Chief, who was now on the scene, ordered police cars to block the road at the starting line to prevent the race from beginning. He ordered Lissa to continue her search with the dog. The two made it all the way back to the starting line before they heard the second device exploding. As soon as the area was cleared, the race was allowed to begin. The runners waved at Lissa and Sheba passed, some blowing kisses of thanks.

The lead story on the six o'clock evening news was the Police Chief commending Officer Mellissa Harding and her canine and the video was repeated on the network news as well. Lissa was at home when she got a call from her dad telling her how proud they were to see her on the news in Tennessee.

Lissa was given a commendation by the Mayor in a ceremony at City Hall and then was named Officer of the Year by the Hamilton County Police Association, an organization made up of the twenty-nine law enforcement agencies in Hamilton County, Ohio.

CHAPTER FOURTEEN

The next several months were mundane after the excitement of the training and then being able to actually utilize it to save lives. The nights passed quickly with Lissa and Sheba playing in the parks and catching an occasional bad guy.

Lissa walked into District One and went to the bulletin board to check on the availability of picking up extra money working an off-duty detail. Cincinnati allows their officers to wear the City uniform and perform security functions for private companies. The officer's hourly pay is established by the Police Department and the location and duties of the security must be approved. The officer then reimburses the City at a rate of five dollars per hour worked to cover the administrative costs of operating the program. On the board was a flyer announcing a Sergeants examination and this time Lissa felt she was ready to move up in her career.

She wrote down the required books from which the test questions would be drawn and vowed to go to the Hamilton County Public Library first thing in the morning to get the study material she would need. There was also a flyer for a new program that the City had instituted for officers who wanted to advance their education. Called "The Master's Program" it would be available to any officer possessing a Bachelor's Degree. The City would pay for the classes and provide the students with City time to study in a group setting. Wanting a degree in Police Administration, Lissa filed a request to be considered.

The Sergeants test was much easier than she anticipated and she was the second one to turn her test in. Every night before roll call, Lissa would check the board for the scores and after a week she found them posted. She scored fifteenth out of the one hundred ten that took the test. Because of the consent decree with the Department of Justice following the riot in Cincinnati in 2001, the City kept two lists for promotion. The second list was minority cops only and Lissa scored first on that list. The consent decree required that, for every four promoted off the primary list, one from the secondary list would also be promoted. That meant that Lissa would receive a promotion as soon as the City promoted four others. Two would be promoted immediately, so she knew that it would only be a few months until her promotion would become reality.

***

The Master's Program at Xavier University was highly regarded around the United States. Lissa was approved to be with five other officers. They attended classes together and met once a week for three hours as a study group.

161

They were paid in compensatory time, which is time off at one and one-half the number of hours. The six would study together and then go to dinner or drinks and she developed a bond with the four males and one other female in the program.

After a study class, Lissa went home to get Sheba and start her shift. After roll call, the two began checking the schools in the City because they were experiencing a high number of breakins. She pulled into the parking lot of Aiken High School in College Hill and immediately saw a car sitting in the lot with exhaust fumes visible due to the cold. That meant the car was running.

She pulled in behind the car and saw the passenger jump out of the car. He immediately began shooting into the police car with some type of automatic weapon. As Lissa scrambled to get out of the car, she could see the bullet holes in the windshield. She took cover behind the door and screamed into the radio, "SHOTS FIRED, SHOTS FIRED, AIKEN HIGH SCHOOL!" Then, concerned that one or more of the bullets might get through to the back seat where Sheba was, she remotely opened the rear door. Instead of coming next to Lissa, Sheba took off at a full run toward the threat to her master. Sheba only made it halfway when she fell to the ground, having been struck by a bullet.

Lissa began frantically shooting back. She fired the Glock until the slide locked back, meaning that she had fired eighteen rounds. She ejected the magazine in her weapon and slammed a new magazine carrying seventeen more bullets. She continued firing, one of the rounds striking the driver in the left shoulder. The driver, now more concerned with his safety than his partner's cover, dropped the car into drive and pulled away leaving the passenger with no cover. As soon as the opening became available, Lissa fired three shots, all of which hit the gunman in the chest. When he hit the ground, Lissa got up and ran, not toward the gunman but toward her best friend who was whimpering softly on the ground.

The first cruiser to arrive to Lissa's call for help was a Ford Expedition with push bumpers. When the cop saw a vehicle driving to get away, the cop hit the car so violently that it turned the car onto its side. Other arriving officers ran to the gunman laying on the ground. A muscular cop ran up to Lissa and pushed her out of the way, picking up Sheba like she was a little doll. The cop carried Sheba back to his cruiser and went screaming out of the parking lot to a twentyfour hour veterinary hospital a little less than four miles away.

Officers dragged the driver, who was screaming in pain, out of the car. Investigators would later determine that Lissa had fired twenty-seven shots and that all of them had hit their intended targets. Twenty-four bullet holes were found in the car and the three that were in a small group in the center of the chest of the second suspect who was very dead.

A female officer ran up to Lissa, who was in a total daze. The female saw blood dripping from Lissa's face which was caused by the flying glass from the driver's window and windshield of the bullet-ridden police car. The female officer wiped away the blood and saw that the injuries were only superficial and let out a sigh of relief.

Police vehicles continued pouring into the parking lot from all directions. The Police Chief, his three Assistant Police Chiefs, the Captain serving as Night Chief and the Commander of District Five all came to the scene. The Chief order Lissa be taken to the hospital to be checked out, stopping the homicide unit from questioning her.

The female officer grabbed Lissa's arm and led her to a cruiser to take her to the hospital. She had to drive through the grass to leave the parking lot as there were police vehicles parked at every entrance to the school. As they pulled onto Llanfair Avenue, Lissa looked at the driver and softly said, "The Chief didn't specify what hospital to take me to, so take me to my dog." The driver made an immediate U-Turn and headed to the veterinary hospital.   ***

The big cop pulled into the parking area of the College Hill Veterinary Clinic. The employees heard the siren wailing outside their entrance and went outside to see what the commotion was.

The cop jumped out of his cruiser and yelled, "A police dog was shot. I need help." He opened the back door of the cruiser and could hear Sheba's breathing was labored and short. He picked the dog up and carried her inside where Dr. Frank Jones, DVM, was waiting at a table. He administered a sedative to Sheba while the staff hooked the dog to oxygen.

The bullet entered Sheba's right upper shoulder stopped next to her heart. The vet cut into Sheba's chest and determined that it would do more harm than good to try to remove the bullet. He ordered the staff to feed blood to replace the amount lost and administered a second dose of sedative to assure that Sheba would not move. He looked at the big cop and said, "I honestly don't know whether or not I can save the dog." The vet saw tears streaming from the cop's face and said, "I am going to do everything possible. That is the best I can offer."

Lissa and her driver pulled into the parking lot where the siren of the other cruiser was still wailing wildly. The driver walked over to the other cruiser and turned off the siren and then went to retrieve Lissa, who sat dazed in the cruiser. The two walked into the clinic and went to where Sheba was laying on a table motionless. Lissa saw the tears in the male cop's eyes and collapsed to the floor. The female who transported Lissa jumped on her radio and called for a paramedic unit for Lissa. The vet administered smelling salts and, when Lissa woke, told her, "Your dog is alive. She suffered a serious wound and the bullet is lodged within an inch of the heart. She is sedated and we will do everything possible for her."

Lissa protested when the paramedics wanted to transport her to University Medical Center, but the male cop said it was not an option and told the paramedics to tie her to the gurney if needed. Lissa was now crying uncontrollably and demanding to stay with her best friend. The male cop looked into her eyes and said, "Your dog will never be alone. She is a brother officer and we will make sure she receives the best care available."

***

The parking lot of the school was the normal chaos that surrounds any major incident. Crime Scene technicians were trying to recover all of the casings fired by both the officer and the dead suspect. The driver of the getaway car was taken to University Medical Center under police guard and the homicide detectives were photographing everything possible. Two tow trucks were called to get the canine cruiser and the getaway car and to take them to the crime lab.

The supervisors had no actual witnesses to the event and there were media trucks everywhere demanding information. The Police Chief held an impromptu press conference where he told the media, "We do not have a lot of information at this point. A police dog was shot and taken to a veterinary hospital and two suspects were shot. One of them was pronounced dead at the scene and the other suffered a non-life threatening injury to the shoulder. We have not yet been able to speak to the police officer as she was taken to the hospital for evaluation. We will have much more information in the morning and will hold a press conference as soon as possible. The extent of the canine's injuries is also unknown at this time."

***

At the hospital Lissa was given a sedative to help her sleep as well. When she awoke, she demanded to know how Sheba was doing. A nurse who was in the room looked startled and asked, "Who is Sheba?" Lissa glared at the nurse and said, "My canine and my BEST FRIEND IN THE WORLD!" The nurse quickly left the room and a Police Captain entered shortly after.

He told Lissa, "Your dog is holding her own. It is a touchand-go situation because of where the bullet ended up. They are keeping her sedated and trying to get her strength rebuilt before they decide whether to try and remove the bullet or leave it where it is. The information I have is that the bullet is lodged next to the dog's heart."

Lissa asked when she would be released and the Captain said, "Right now if you are up to it." Lissa nodded that she was ready to leave. The Captain said, "I know that you are concerned about your canine and there is not a doubt that this is a good shoot, but the homicide people still need to get your statement.

If you don't feel up to talking to them now, I will make sure they delay for a bit. Would you like to be with your dog at the moment?" Lissa simply replied, "Please."

The Captain left the room and moments later the nurse returned with Lissa's blood covered uniform. Lissa only dressed enough to cover her body and walked out of the room where another female officer was waiting. The officer said, "Hi, my name is Officer Doris Hendricks and I have orders to take you wherever you need to go." Lissa said, "I need to go to my house in Mount Lookout to get clothes and then I need to get to the vet hospital to be with my dog."

After a quick stop at Lissa's house, the two went to the clinic. The vet looked at Lissa and said, "You have a dog with a strong will. It is likely that she will survive, but her days as a working dog are over. I had to leave the bullet where it is. She will be able to be a pet and play and do the normal things that a dog can do. But the grueling life of a police canine would likely cause the bullet to move and that would likely kill her. Would you like to see her? She is awake?" Lissa followed the vet to a treatment room where there was still a uniformed police officer standing guard. Sheba's eyes lit up when she saw Lissa and Lissa had to move fast to stop the dog from trying to jump off the table. Lissa hugged Sheba and rubbed the dog's face and ears. The vet gave the dog another shot to sleep and told Lissa to return tomorrow and she could take the dog home.

The driver then took Lissa to CIS to be interviewed by the homicide detectives. As she entered the secured area of CIS, veteran detectives all wanted to know how her canine was doing. Robin ran up and hugged Lissa and asked about Sheba as well. The two homicide detectives took Lissa into an interview room and the Sergeant said, "If you look at the camera, the red light is not on yet. We wanted you to know up front that this is only a formality. Are you mentally okay to do this now?" Lissa nodded and the other detective threw the switch that turned on the audio and video. It took almost four hours for Lissa to walk them through the event. One commented that they had never experienced such a detailed recollection of a critical event.

Lissa was put on paid administrative leave, a standard procedure when a police officer is involved in a use of deadly force. She would be required to see the police psychologist to be cleared to return to work, but their office did not have an available time for four days.

Lissa took the time to spend with Sheba helping her recover from the gunshot wound that the dog suffered. She was relaxing with Sheba when her phone rang. The caller told Lissa that the commander of the canine unit wanted to see her as soon as possible. Lissa called Liza, who had just gotten off her midnight shift and asked her to come sleep at her house so that Sheba would have someone present. Liza arrived about thirty minutes later and Lissa told her to climb into her bed while Lissa went to the meeting with the commander. Liza waited until Lissa left before moving to the bedroom and laughed when Sheba followed her and laid down in her bed at the foot of the big bed. Liza slowly climbed out of the bed and sat down on the floor, softly scratching Sheba's ears and petting her until the dog relaxed and went to sleep. Then she quietly crawled back into the big bed and fell asleep quickly.

Lissa arrived at the Special Operations headquarters and knocked on the Lieutenant's door. The Lieutenant motioned her into his office and told her to close the door. He said, "I just received the report from the vet that Sheba is physically incapable of being a working dog. That leaves us with two options. We can get you a new dog and put Sheba down or we can transfer you out of the unit and retire your dog, which means you would get to keep her." Without hesitation, Lissa said, "Sheba is my family. There is no way that I would let anyone put her down. I have loved my time here, but this is a no-brainer." The Lieutenant smiled and said, "That is what I expected to hear, but I had to give you the option. I will put in the transfer papers back to patrol. The transfer will take effect when you return to work."

***

Lissa arrived for her appointment fifteen minutes early and was surprised when the receptionist told her the doctor was waiting for her. She was taken to a room and told to pick the comfortable chair of her choice. The doctor came into the room and said, "You realize that you are now a one percenter, don't you?" Lissa asked, "What the hell does that mean?" The doctor replied, "Less than one percent of American cops are involved in more than one deadly force encounter. This is your second." He continued, "What can you tell me about this encounter?" Lissa looked into the doctor's eyes and said, "Everything.   I spent four hours walking the shooting investigators through every step." The doctor next asked, "What were your feelings after this shooting?" Lissa thought for a second and answered, "I truly felt nothing. The asshole left me no choice because my cruiser was riddled with bullets and he shot my dog. When the opportunity came, I fired until he went to the ground, then ran and checked on my canine. I was just told that Sheba is not physically capable of returning to the street and will be retired. I am being transferred out of the Canine Unit and will be returning to the street as soon as you clear me. The doctor next asked how her dog was doing and Lissa replied, "Her name is Sheba. She is moving around the house slowly and her appetite is not what it should be, but she is healing at a pace I am told is normal." The doctor smiled and said, "I will notify the Police Chief that you are ready to return to work. Be safe and don't come visit me unless it is of your choice!"

***

Lissa got the call she was waiting for from the Chief's office, but it was not what she expected to hear. The secretary told her that her promotion had come through and that she would need to take her uniforms to Roy Tailor Uniform Company to have her stripes sewn on and then be at City Hall for the swearing in ceremony. Lissa hung up the phone and immediately called her parents to see if they would be able to attend the ceremony. At the ceremony, Lissa stood with three males who had also been promoted. Her parents hugged her and told her how proud they were of her. Her brother could not get off of work and was unable to make the trip, but sent a card that said, "To the best sister anyone could have. I am proud of what you have done."

***

Lissa spent three weeks at the Police Academy taking classes on Leadership. Part of the training was actually reading the collective bargaining agreement between the City and the union. She was told that cops would file grievances which would result in arbitration if the Sergeants did not understand what was in the agreement and what the procedure was to take disciplinary action.

The new Sergeants were given their new assignments. Lissa would be working as a third shift supervisor in District Four, which covers the north end of the City.

She arrived for her first shift as a supervisor almost onehalf hour early. She asked the desk officer where she would find her locker and was sent to the basement of the building. She was surprised when she entered the female locker room and found her name already on a locker. She stored her gear and went back upstairs to the Supervisors office. There were two desks in the cramped room. At one desk sat a large frame man who appeared to be in his mid-sixties. He stood up, extended his hand, and said, "My name is Willis Woodson and I am the senior Sergeant in the Police Department. I have forty-seven years in this job and I must have pissed someone off along the way because I get to potty train the new kids who think they can be a boss.

Just do what I tell you to do when I tell you to do it and you will avoid having to take your uniforms back to have those stripes removed." He pointed to a thick file lying on the other desk and said, "That is yours. You need to read each of those reports that the cops wrote and either sign off on them or return them. We have cops who can't spell, can't write, or just too damn lazy to write any information. There are red pens in the right hand drawer. Mark whatever needs to be re-written and then put the report in the bin marked 'return' or sign the report at the bottom and put it the 'out' bin. Before you start on that, we need to conduct your first roll call".

When the two walked into the roll call room, Lissa thought she was in a zombie convention. The twelve cops in the room looked like they hadn't slept in days. Sgt. Woodson yelled out loud enough that it scared Lissa, "Get off your dead asses, NOW!" The cops sprung out of their chairs and stood at attention because they knew better than to pee in this Sergeant's Wheaties.

Woodson and Lissa walked to the front of the room and the old geezer said, "This is Sgt. Harding. She will be working thirds with me. Any cop with half a brain knows better than to cause a delay in my potty training because your miserable existence will deteriorate faster than you can fart." He grabbed Lissa's arm and the two walked down the line of cops who had their weapon in one hand and the magazine in the other. The cops were in short sleeve shirts for their summer uniform, so they were not required to wear a tie. Woodson walked up to a thirtyish male and asked, "Do you actually change shirts more than once a month?" The other cops in line snickered and the male cop said absolutely nothing.

Woodson read off the crimes from the previous sixteen hours and gave out the radio assignments for the night and told them to go out and actually catch a few bad guys for a change. The cops filed out of the room and Lissa went back to open the thick file and get started. It took almost two hours for her to get through the reports for the one day. She had marked more than half of them for a problem which made the report useless.

When she was done, Woodson motioned her to get up and the two walked out to a cruiser. Woodson rode her around the District pointing out the hot spots where the shootings and mayhem were commonplace. He took her to the intersection of Liberty and Vine, which is just on the north end of the downtown area and stopped the police car. He pointed to the south side and said "That is in District One, the northwest corner is in District Five and the Northeast is ours. When I started on this job there was a White Castle restaurant on the southeast corner and on Friday and Saturday nights, a police car went through this intersection every one minute between eight p.m. and four a.m. Thank God they tore it down."

As they continued riding, he told her, "A boss is required on every dead body call, use of force incident, and when any citizen demands a supervisor respond." Before she knew it, the night was over and her head was spinning with all of the information. As they prepared to call it a night Woodson quipped, "The good news is that they start newbies on a Sunday. That is the slowest night of the week. Lissa drove home and found Sheba lying in wait by the front door for her master to get home.

***

The days and weeks passed quickly. Lissa was developing the respect of the people under her with the exception of one veteran cop who wouldn't answer his radio when

175

communications called. Lissa stopped at a United Dairy Farmers convenience and picked up two cups of coffee. She then called for the problem cop to meet her in a parking lot. When he arrived, she handed one of the cups out of her window to the cop and said, "Did I do something to piss you off?" The old cop got a funny look on his face and said, "No." Lissa then asked, "Then why are you trying to make me look bad?" The old cop said simply, "I'm not trying to make you look bad." Lissa continued, "When you don't answer your radio runs, other cops think they don't have to answer their calls either. I am told that you have enough time to retire and that, if anyone pushes you, you will just pull the pin. If your goal is to make me look bad, you are succeeding, but that shit is gonna stop because I will make every day until you retire miserable. Are we clear?" The cop nodded that he understood and Lissa drove away. She never had another problem with the cop.

***

It was four twenty on Monday morning when Lissa received a call in the Supervisor office. The caller was Police Communications who said that they had been unable to reach a female officer running beat 4302. The caller said that they had been calling the officer for over an hour. Lissa walked out of the District and drove to the officer's assigned area looking for the cruiser without success. Almost as an afterthought, Lissa used the City issued cell phone and called Communications, asking them to look up the officer's home address. They came back with the address, which was located in District Four. Lissa thought the officer might have gone home for lunch and the battery in her portable radio might have gone dead. When she arrived at the home, sure enough there was a police car parked in the driveway, but it was weird that there was not a single light on inside the house.

Lissa walked up to the door and knocked, but no answer. She knocked harder and still got no response. Using her flashlight, she banged on the door until lights started coming on. The officer answered the door wearing a nightgown and looking like she had been asleep. Lissa ordered her to drive directly to the District. Lissa was really pissed at this point and used the cell phone to call communications to have the Night Chief meet her at District Four. Night Chief duties rotate among the Captains in the Police Department. The rotation had fallen on Captain Newville, the commander of District Three. The officer sauntered into the District and Lissa pointed her to an interview room and told her to wait. When Captain Newhall walked into the District, Lissa laid out what she had found. The two walked into the interview room and the Captain said, "Leave your gun belt and badge on the table. You are immediately suspended pending a disciplinary hearing." When the female started to protest, Captain Newville put his finger to his mouth and said, "Shhhh, not a word. cry to the union or get a lawyer, I really don't care. More importantly, get out of my police station."

***

177

Lissa continued to work toward her Master's degree in Police Administration. She had become friends with the five other members of her study group. She was reaching the point where she would start working with her advisor on her thesis and had several ideas for a topic. She considered "The DOJ war on police agencies" and "A multidiscipline approach to sexual assault." She was leaning toward the latter because it was a program that she might be able to convince the Police Department to implement. Her advisor appeared, from her discussions, to be very liberal in his ideology and he was not going to be easy to convince that there actually was anything wrong with the DOJ selectively targeting law enforcement agencies for Civil Rights violations. The two had numerous arguments about Ferguson, Missouri and the Staten Island, New York incidents. She believed that he was actually anti-police.

***

Lissa was out riding around the District because it was a Friday night. A call for help came from the University of Cincinnati Police, who were in foot pursuit of an escapee from the Psych Unit of the hospital. She heard car after car acknowledge that they were responding and quietly prayed that the cops would not run into each other trying to get there. The chase wound through the Corryville area which abuts the UC Campus and the hospital. Lissa heard that the cops had the suspect pinned in a driveway on Eden Street. As she was pulling up to the scene, she heard three gunshots. She ran to the entrance to the driveway and saw at least fifteen cops with their guns drawn. The suspect was on the pavement of the driveway and was still breathing. In the confusion that followed, she was able to determine that one Cincinnati officer had fired two shots and a University cop fired one. The paramedic arrived and advised that all three wounds were likely lethal, one hitting the femoral artery, one was a groin shot and the third was center of the chest.

She looked at the cops who actually fired the shots and said, "You want an attorney, correct?" Her head was bobbing up and down signaling that they should answer 'yes.' A Lieutenant arrived moments later and immediately asked what the officers had told her. She looked at the Lieutenant and said, "Sir, they both invoked their right to counsel, so I was unable to ask them any questions. Cops who were simply witnesses told the same story. When the suspect realized he had cornered himself, he picked up a brick and ran toward the three cops blocking his only escape route at full speed. He screamed, "Kill me, Kill me!" Lissa ordered two cops to get crime scene tape and tape off almost a full block for the crime scene technicians and the detectives. As the Cincinnati officer was being taken to a car to be transported to the Homicide Unit, he whispered to Lissa, "Thanks boss" as he passed her. Since the University cop was not technically under the control of Cincinnati Police, he was taken to Homicide by a University Police Lieutenant.

She was still at the scene at ten o'clock in the morning as the technicians collected the brick, shell casings and a drawing with the positions of the fifteen different cops. While there, they learned the six-foot seven-inch, two hundred eighty pound suspect had just gotten out of jail the previous afternoon and got arrested by a suburban police department for shoplifting.

When he began to act crazy in the Springdale Police headquarters, they took him to the Medical Center for a psych evaluation. The suspect seemed to know that the jail would not accept a person exhibiting mental illness and that he would be able to walk away from the locked unit first thing in the morning. His opportunity came in the early morning, but he didn't anticipate that a University cop would recognize him as he tried to leave the hospital.
The suspect died the next day.

CHAPTER FIFTEEN

Lissa had been a supervisor in District Four for a little over six months when she was asked if she would like to transfer into the Police Integrity Unit, which is the Internal Investigation Unit for the Police Department. She was told that the position was a stepping-stone to promotions and that all of the Assistant Chiefs and most of the Captains had come through the Integrity Unit. The people who worked in the unit were hated by cops who called them "The Rat Squad" and "Headhunters." She found herself in a quandary because she wanted to be liked by other cops, but the idea of keeping the trust of the public by cleaning out the bad cops won out. She accepted.

Her first case was a complaint from a District One Lieutenant who stopped a police explorer coming into the District for a ride. The explorer was obviously wearing a bulletproof vest and the Lieutenant demanded to know how he was able to acquire it. The young man said he bought it from a District One cop named Roy Heter, a twelve-year veteran. The Lieutenant ordered the explorer to take the vest off and looked for a City of Cincinnati identification number on the rear plate. Sure enough, the number showed.   Lissa went to the Police Department Supply Unit to verify that the vest did belong to the City and, if so, to find out who it was issued to. She was told that the vest was issued to Heter and that he had filed a request for a new vest claiming that the old one had been taken from the back seat of his car. Lissa called Heter into the Integrity Unit and confronted him with the facts, which he vehemently

denied. When he said he wanted to have legal counsel present, the interview was immediately terminated. Lissa took the information to the Hamilton County Prosecutor, who presented it to a Grand Jury. The
Grand Jury issued an indictment for the crime of Theft in Office, a felony crime in Ohio. The law says that any theft offense, inconsequential of the value of the item taken, while working as a public employee is guilty of the offense.

With the indictment in hand, Lissa and two other Integrity Unit investigators went to the District for the third shift roll call. They walked directly to Heter and advised him he was under arrest. After removing his gun belt, Heter was taken out of the roll call room in handcuffs to the gasps of the room full of cops.

***

Lissa took the time to check on the status of the officer she had found sleeping in her home while still on duty. The female had been fired by the Police Department, but the union had filed for arbitration. The arbitrator ruled that the officer should be reinstated because she had suffered Post-Partum depression after having a child. Six months after being reinstated, the officer was charged with Receiving Stolen Property when a stolen bicycle was found in her back yard.

The Captain of the Unit posted a promotional examination for the position of Police Lieutenant and he urged Lissa to apply to take the test, even though she had only been a Sergeant for a little more than one year.

***

Lissa liked the idea of not having to wear a uniform to work. She had several pants suits that accentuated her slim figure. She showed up for her shift and found a new folder on her desk. It was a complaint from a prostitute that alleged she had been stopped by a District Five uniformed officer, who ran a warrant check and determined that she had an outstanding misdemeanor warrant for soliciting prostitution.

He handcuffed her and placed her in the back of the patrol car and, instead of taking her to the Justice Center, took her to a dead end street and told her he would let her go if she sucked his dick. Not wanting to go to jail, she told him to open his pants. Without taking the handcuffs off of her, he unzipped his pants and told her to open her mouth wide. When he was deep into her mouth, he ordered her to close her mouth around his member and to suck it until he shot his load. When he was done, he zipped up his pants and removed the handcuffs. He drove away leaving her to walk back to where he had picked her up.

Lissa looked at the time and date and called the Captain of District Five, telling him that she needed the roster for the second relief on that day. She got photos of all the cops

183

working and then went to the Justice Center to interview the hooker. The hooker immediately picked out a black cop whose name was Dwight Tobin. As she was leaving, Lissa asked the hooker how she ended up in jail if the cop released her. The hooker told her that she returned to her spot and within ten minutes another cop pulled up. This one took her directly to jail and that was why she ratted on the first cop.

Lissa called District Five and told the Captain to order Officer Tobin to report to the Integrity Unit as soon as he arrived for work. Tobin got into the office just after three o'clock and Lissa took him to an interview room. She read the statement of the hooker and Tobin said, "I don't know anything about it." Lissa could immediately tell from his body language that he was lying, so she said, "Here is the deal, pal. I am going to get the computer records from your shift that day and we will see if you ran a wanted check on this woman." Tobin scowled and said, "I think I want a lawyer, now." Lissa told him he was free to return to his District. As he started out the door Lissa quipped, "Look in the mirror a lot asshole because I will be back there at some point."

Even though the computer records corroborated the statements of the hooker, the Prosecutor's Office said that they did not have enough to take the case to a Grand Jury. Lissa called Tobin back into the Integrity Unit office and read him his Garrity Rights. <u>Garrity v New Jersey</u> is a United States Supreme Court case that says that a public employee can be ordered to truthfully answer questions, but that the information gained from those questions cannot be used in a criminal trial. Where the <u>Miranda</u> warnings are a constitutional protection, <u>Garrity</u> warnings are not because it is an administrative tool.

Lissa placed the form with the warnings printed on it and read them to the officer out loud. Once she finished, Tobin said, "Let me tell you about the other six women I did the same thing with." Shocked, Lissa asked, "What six women?" Tobin related each of the contacts with women where he got sexual favors in exchange for not taking them to jail. Tobin was savvy enough to know that no criminal case could be brought and he was about to be fired anyway. Tobin was told to leave his gun belt and his badge on the table and was escorted out of the building and driven back to the District to clean out his locker. Lissa completed the case investigation form disgusted that she could not check the box that said 'closed by arrest', but had to check the box marked 'closed by other'.

***

Lissa found that, except for Liza and Robin, she was being snubbed by other cops because she was an IA rat. She tried to tell several that she was not looking for cops to jam up, but her statements fell on deaf ears. She had difficulty understanding why cops would back up pieces of garbage like Tobin, but just learned to ignore their sneering and then avoiding the normal cop hangouts.

The Lieutenant's test was significantly more difficult than the Sergeant test and Lissa did not have a good feeling as she walked out of the testing room. When the scores were finally posted by Civil Service, she had passed the test but was forty-second on the full list and fourth on the minority list. That meant twelve from the main list would have to be promoted before she would make Lieutenant.

***

Lissa began to notice that every day as she dressed Sheba would be waiting by the front door as if she was ready to get back to work. Because she had accrued a lot of time, Lissa put in for a week's vacation and decided to take Sheba to visit her parents.

Lissa and Sheba piled into the car and headed south on Interstate 75 toward Tennessee.

Almost as an afterthought, Lissa jumped off the exit for London, Kentucky to stop and visit Donny and see how he was doing. She drove up to the house where the family lived only to find that the house was empty with a for sale sign in the front yard. Lissa drove to the Police Department and asked to see the Assistant Chief with whom she had dealt. He smiled as he came to the front of the building and told Lissa that they were sorry to hear that she had left the AG's Office.

He asked, "How can the London Police Department help you today?" Lissa told him that she had gone to Donny's house only to find that they had moved and asked, "Is there any way you can get me a valid address? I just wanted to stop on my way to Tennessee to see how he is doing." After waiting about ten minutes in the waiting area, the Assistant Chief returned with a sheet of paper showing their new address and directions on how to get there.

Lissa shook the Assistant Chief's hand and thanked him and went back to her car. She followed the directions and pulled up in front of a house where Donny and his sisters were playing in the front yard. This house was much nicer than the one they had been in and the children were clean and well dressed. Lissa hadn't gotten more than two steps from her car when Donny saw her and yelled out, "Mommy, Mommy, come quick! Guess who is here?" Donny ran full speed, jumping into Lissa's arms causing Sheba to come out of the car at a run.

Lissa gave a command and Sheba immediately sat down next to her Master. Lissa told Donny, "This is my police dog and her name is Sheba." Donny bent down and hugged Sheba, who was loving the attention from the child. The two girls also came over and Sheba rolled over and the four played in the grass while Lissa chatted with Donny's mom. Donny's mom told Lissa that Donny had been attending counseling and was beginning to get over the horrific events that had been inflicted upon him. She told Lissa that she had gone back to school and was now working as a Licensed Practical Nurse at a local nursing home. With the extra income, she had been able to get them a better house in a better neighborhood. The two chatted for more than an hour while Sheba kept the children entertained, chasing anything the kids would throw.

Lissa hugged everyone and said she and Sheba were traveling to Tennessee and needed to get going. There were tears as she and Sheba got back into the car, but Lissa felt an inner peace that Donny would be okay.

Sheba and Lissa arrived at the house in Lafollette in the late afternoon. Sheba walked around the yard as if she were searching for something, checking out every bush and shrub. Lissa's mom came out and jumped, because she had never actually seen the large German Shepard before. Lissa laughed and called Sheba over to meet her parents. Once again, the dog laid down and showed her belly, telling everyone that she wanted to be scratched. After dinner was done, Lissa took Sheba outside and her parents watched as the two played with a tennis ball.

Lissa's mom said that her brother had moved out of the house with his new girlfriend, but that little else changed in the small town. Lissa told her parents that she would be going to the Police Department to say "hi" to the people who got her into law enforcement.

It was a relaxation that both Sheba and Lissa needed. Sheba was not nearly as antsy about not being a working dog any longer and appeared to relish her retirement. Sheba was really turning into a people dog. The two rode down to the Police Department and as they were approaching the main entrance, Sheba froze and laid down, looking at a backpack sitting by the front door. Lissa walked into the station and told the desk officer, who she had never seen before, that she was a Cincinnati, Ohio cop and that her explosive trained canine had just 'hit' on a suspicious package outside. The desk officer, thinking this lady was just another nut case, called the Police Chief who came running out. He took one look at Lissa and ordered the officer to call the bomb squad immediately. Twenty minutes later, the Tennessee Bureau of Investigation Bomb detection team arrived. They did an x-ray on the package and determined that it was, in fact, an explosive. They carefully removed it from the entrance and took it to a field where they detonated it. The explosion left a three foot hole in the ground from the force of the blast.

The Police Chief thanked Lissa profusely for saving the lives of the local cops. He told Lissa that he would be writing a letter of commendation to the Cincinnati Police Chief. The local paper got a picture of Lissa and Sheba which ran on the front page the next day. Lissa was now a local hero. The City Council also wanted to recognize her, but their meeting was not scheduled until after she had to be back to work in Cincinnati.

Lissa and Sheba would sit on the porch of the quiet town until late at night just relaxing and enjoying the peace and serenity. After dealing with the urban world, this was a great change of

pace. They regretted having to leave after only a few days, but
the realities of the real world were calling.

CHAPTER SIXTEEN

On Lissa's first day back, she was told to report to the Lieutenant's office. The Lieutenant told her to go see the Commander of the Regional Drug Unit and was provided the address of their office. The office was in the rear of an empty warehouse just west of the downtown area.

When Lissa arrived at the location, she was directed to the office of Paul Gutterie, who pointed to a chair for her to sit. He told her that a Cincinnati Police Officer named George Pillar had come in for an interview to become a member of the drug task force. At the conclusion of the interview Pillar was told that he needed to schedule a time for a polygraph examination which was the final step in joining the unit. Pillar told Gutterie that he changed his mind and was no longer interested in joining and then abruptly left. Gutterie had a gut instinct that there was a lot more to this story and wanted Lissa to investigate.

Lissa returned to her office and called Pillar's commanding officer to schedule him to come into the Integrity Unit for a meeting. When Pillar arrived, he looked extremely nervous and Lissa instantly knew that the drug commander was correct in his assumption. She asked Pillar what caused him to change his mind about joining the drug task force. His reply was, "It no longer sounded like something I wanted to do." Lissa asked,

"Why did you wait until the lie detector was brought up to change your mind?" Pillar hemmed and hawed trying to formulate an answer but finally said, "I just changed my mind. That is all you need to know."

Lissa said, "Wait here," and went to the Lieutenant's office to find out how he wanted to proceed. The Lieutenant told her to Rule 26 him, which is the administration of *Garrity Warnings*. Garrity is the name of the United States Supreme Court decision that requires public employees to truthfully answer any and all questions asked of them or face termination of their employment.

Lissa returned to the interview room where Pillar was left waiting. She read the warnings to him at which point he told her, "I planted marijuana on a suspect five years ago." He went on to say that, "The guy already had marijuana in his possession when he got arrested and I just added the amount I had found earlier in the day to his stash. It saved me having to turn it in separately as evidence."

Lissa then told Pillar that he was suspended pending disciplinary action and asked for his badge and his gun. Pillar dutifully removed the .40 caliber handgun from its holster and laid it on the table. Then he removed his Cincinnati Police badge from his shirt and laid it next to the gun.

Two weeks later he disciplinary hearing was held before the Captain of District One and lasted a very short time. The Captain recommended to the Chief that Pillar be fired and his decision was signed off by the Police Chief. The union, under the collective bargaining agreement with the City, immediately announced it would be filing for an arbitration hearing.

Lissa was told to provide all of the information of her investigation to the County Prosecutor's Office, who were contemplating criminal charges of Tampering with Evidence, a felony crime in Ohio. Lissa looked at her supervisor and proclaimed, "*Garrity* does not allow the introduction of any information we gained to be used in a criminal action", but she was told that was not her problem. She delivered the packet to the Prosecutor and was shocked when, two days later, an indictment of the officer was announced to the media.

CHAPTER SEVENTEEN

As the months passed, Lissa was mostly handling administrative rule violations cases for the Unit. She wanted to put together a pro-active approach to test the loyalty of the officers sworn to protect the people of Cincinnati.

She presented her concept at a Unit meeting. Calling it an "in Check," students from the University of Cincinnati would be given a wallet containing one hundred dollars in cash and a driver's license. They would stand on a street corner and flag down the first police vehicle that passed by. The wallet would be given to the officer and it would be tracked all the way to the property room. The test would be to see if anyone removed any of the cash from the wallet.

She argued that if the contents of the wallet remained intact, it would signal the honesty of the members of the police department. It would also identify dishonest cops and allow the department to prosecute officers who violated the trust that they were given. When the Captain questioned the defense of "entrapment," Lissa offered this explanation. "It is not entrapment to offer the opportunity to commit a crime. Entrapment is when you also give them the tools to commit that crime. Lissa was told to recruit the students and write the protocols for the program.

Over the next seven months, the program was run in all areas of the City. Of the eighty-seven times that the "test" was conducted, only two of those resulted in missing money. Criminal indictments were obtained against both of the officers and they were fired from the Police Department.

****

Lissa was working feverishly with her academic advisor on her Master's thesis. She had developed a multidisciplinary sexual assault response program which would involve law enforcement, mental health professionals, advocacy groups and medical professionals. One member of each group would be assigned to a team and they would remain with the victim from inception to completion.

Lissa also received a "heads-up" that she was at the top of the Lieutenant's list and her promotion would be coming within weeks. She was beginning to tire of being a cop who investigated only other cops. She was ready to move onto other challenges in law enforcement.

Her notification of her promotion came with her transfer to head of the Personal Crimes

Section. She called Robin Miller to meet her for dinner so that she could tell her the news that Robin had been right when she told Lissa, "Someday you will be my boss!"

Prior to her first day in the new position Lissa was called to the Police Chief's Office. He told her that he had read her thesis and was impressed by the concept. He told her that forming this coalition would be her first task at the Personal Crimes Unit.

Lissa started by calling the Women Helping Women group and getting them onboard. Lissa told them that their task would be to provide a representative who would be with a victim from the initial interview through trial. The second call was to the University of Cincinnati Psych Unit to get psychologists and psychiatrists who would be willing to avail themselves to a victim on an as-needed basis. The last call was to the Greater Cincinnati Mental Health Association to enlist their services to assign a single person to monitor the mental health of the victim and then stay with that victim until the trial was over.

The civilians were easy to sell on this program. It was going to be much tougher to get the cops to buy into it. For that Lissa enlisted the help of Robin to sell it to the other investigators.

At the initial meeting of the heads of the participating agencies, they identified a problem that would need to be solved for this program to work. The Health Insurance Portability Act (better known as HIPPA) protects the privacy of medical information of patients and the medical professionals involved would not be able to share any information to the investigators without obtaining a search warrant. Lissa went to the City Law

Department and asked them to draft a waiver that victims could sign, but they declined to get involved. Unwavering in her commitment to make this work, she contacted the Administrator of University Medical Center who said he would have his Legal Department find a way to make it work. It took several days, but the hospital lawyers created a document that a victim or a parent or guardian could sign that would allow the exchange of all information between the team members.

The administrative team decided to start with one team and then develop more teams if the first was successful.

The first case that the program was implemented threw a wrench into the well-oiled machine because it involved the rape of a twelve-year-old girl. The University of Cincinnati Psych Unit made a call to Children's Hospital and got their involvement. While the Children's people worked with the child, the U.C. people worked with the parents of the victim. Unlike most cases of this type, the perpetrator was not a relative and the attack occurred during the day when the young girl was walking home from school. The team met weekly to discuss the aspects of the case, which moved slowly because there were no known suspects. Lissa sat in on the first few meetings, setting up a police artist to sit with the young girl, the advocate and the mental health professional. DNA had been gotten off the child's dress, but there was no match in the national database. Having the medical professionals keeping contact with the victim and her family kept the situation from deteriorating while the investigators worked feverishly to identify the suspect. The team met weekly to keep on top of the physical and mental needs of the victim and to keep her parents informed of the status of the police investigation. The adult psych people worked with the parents while Children's Hospital handled the child. The team felt that this clearly was making a horrific situation bearable for the victim and her family.

Lissa stayed in constant contact with the progress of the first team and the administrative team decided to form three other teams. The teams would get their cases based upon the rotation of the police investigators. As soon as the case was assigned to a Personal Crimes team, they would initiate the other members of their team.

The second case that fell into the program was one that Lissa took a personal interest in. It involved the rape of a ten-year-old boy who was unwilling to identify the offender. He had been brought to Children's Hospital because of stomach pains. An examination of his anal cavity showed tearing and he was impacted. When the file hit her desk Lissa immediately thought of Donny, the young boy she worked with when she was with the Kentucky Attorney General. She drove home and picked up Sheba and took the canine to the hospital with her. Sheba's eyes perked up as they approached Lissa's unmarked police car because the dog knew it was time to go to work again.

Lissa asked for the meeting to be held in the play room, just as she had done with Donny. The young boy was seated on the floor playing with the toys when Lissa and the large German Shepard walked in. Lissa introduced herself and Sheba and asked, "And what is your name?" Without looking up from the toys, the young boy answered simply "Marty." Lissa looked down at the dog and said, "Sheba, go say hello to Marty." Sheba very slowly walked over to Marty, whose eyes got wider with each step. The dog gently licked the boy's face and walked around him and laid down placing her head on his leg. Lissa looked and said, "Marty, she loves her head scratched." The boy began scratching the dog's head and Sheba rolled over on her back with her legs extended upward. The boy instinctively began scratching Sheba's stomach and intently watched the face of the dog, seeing that she was enjoying every minute. While the two played, Lissa told an investigator to go to McDonald's and get the child a kid's meal. She sat on the floor with him while he ate and then she asked, "Marty, can you tell me who hurt you?"   Tears began streaming down the young boy's face as he said simply, "Daddy."

Lissa asked, Can you tell me what daddy did to you?" The boy answered, "It started three weeks ago. Daddy came to my bed and slipped my pants down. He put oil on a toothbrush handle and slid it into my butt. It didn't hurt, but it also didn't feel good. Over the next days the thing he put up my butt got bigger. Two nights ago he put his thing in and it really hurt bad! He put in deep up my butt and then grunted. I cried and he left my room. The next day I couldn't poop and my tummy started hurting real bad. That was when mom took me to the hospital."

Lissa looked directly into the boy's face and said, "I promise you that daddy will never ever hurt you again. We need to go so give Sheba a nice smooch. She will like that." The boy smiled and picked up Sheba's face, but the dog was licking his face so fast, he could not react. Lissa looked at the investigator as she walked out of the room and said, "Take a SWAT team and kick that sonofabitch's front door down and hope that he resists!"

As the weeks and months passed, Lissa program was receiving national acclaim. She had received calls from Boston, Los Angeles, New York, Chicago, Tampa and Philadelphia Police Departments asking her to come to their cities and help them develop it. The Ohio Peace Officer Training Commission, the training arm of the Ohio Attorney General, offered to host a conference at their academy outside Columbus, Ohio and the Police Chief signed off on it. He also told Lissa that he had placed her name to attend the National Academy at the FBI Academy.

The program is by invitation only and consists of sixteen weeks of intense training for management level local law enforcement. The program is attended by police managers from every urban agency in the U.S. and many other countries. The selection process is that each Assistant U.S. Attorney gets one seat to give out. Lissa was surprised when she received the twenty-two page application for the seat given to the Southern Ohio Office. As she filled out the detailed questions, she felt like she was applying for a job. She received her acceptance letter ten weeks later.

CHAPTER EIGHTEEN

Lissa was glad that Liza agreed to keep Sheba while Lissa was in Virginia. She would not be able to make the trip back and forth on the weekends because of the expense. She knew that Liza loved the dog almost as much as Lissa.

She flew into Reagan International Airport on Saturday night and then drove the forty miles into Virginia via I-95. There would be a dinner for the attendees on Sunday evening and she wanted to be ready for it. When she registered, she was provided with a course summary which identified the topics to be discussed. They included: Police Staffing and Scheduling, Writing a Budget, Managing a Training Unit, Managing an Investigative Unit, Effective Use of Tactical Teams, and Team Building Skills.

As she walked around the room where the dinner was being held, she was impressed by the nametags identifying people as Chief, Colonel, Lieut. Colonel, Inspector, Commander and Captain. She wanted to hide the fact that she was only a Lieutenant. She saw students from major police organizations as well as a number from international police agencies.

On the first day of the class, she found herself seated next to a Bolivian Police Chief, who had an interpreter seated next to him because he spoke no English. The group of one hundred eighty cops was broken into three separate classes of sixty. When it came her turn to introduce herself, she stood up and said, "My name is Lieut. Melissa Harding and I am the Personal Crimes Unit Commander for the Cincinnati, Ohio Police Department.

The days were packed with learning and the nights spent studying. She joined a study group that consisted of an LAPD Captain, an NYPD Inspector, a female Deputy Chief from Oshkosh, Wisconsin PD, and a Metro Dade Lt. Colonel. They met after dinner each evening to discuss the day's lesson and to make notes for the multiple tests that are given throughout the program.

She particularly enjoyed the demonstrations, which included bomb detonation and deploying tactical teams. She got to watch the renowned FBI Special Response Team handle a simulated terrorist raid. Her class also got to watch training in the famed "Hogan's Alley." In its original form, it was a sidewalk with facades on both sides that FBI agents were required to walk. Targets would appear on each side and the agents were required to only shoot bad guys without hitting hostages or passersby. It had transitioned into a village with paved streets and a business district. All of the buildings served as FBI classrooms. The first time she walked into the area, she froze to read the sign at the entrance.

It said, "WELCOME TO HOGAN'S ALLEY.

WARNING, if you are stopped by a law enforcement officer, comply fully."

By week sixteen, Lissa felt as though she had been beaten with a baseball bat. The intensity of the training was palpable and the amount learned invaluable. She just really wanted to get back home.

CHAPTER NINETEEN

Upon her return from the class, Lissa decided that it was time to join a professional law enforcement organization to plan for her future. She chose the International Association of Chiefs of Police, a group with thirty-three thousand members worldwide. As their requirements for active member status require the rank of Lieutenant or above, she thought it would be a perfect fit.

Upon receiving her first copy of their monthly magazine, *Police Chief*, Lissa decided to write an article detailing the success of her pilot program. She wrote a case study of Marty, detailing the investigation and mental health services provided. She noted that upon the sentencing of the father to life in prison, the police investigation and the victim advocate participation had been completed. More importantly, the mental health services were continued pro bono with no end date set. After the article was published, Lissa was contacted by the IACP asking if she would be willing to make a presentation at the annual conference to be held in Phoenix, Arizona in October. Conference expenses and travel would be paid for by the IACP.

Lissa forwarded the request to the Police Chief and received a reply two days later. It said that she was being detailed to the convention, meaning that she would be paid by the City for her time at the convention.

Lissa landed at the Phoenix International Airport the day before the conference was scheduled to begin. The uniformed police presence at the Airport was overwhelming. Everywhere she looked there was a contingent of uniformed officers and she was not sure why.

She checked into the hotel where the IACP had put her and, once again, saw a large number of cops just standing around. When she awoke the next morning, a copy of the *Arizonan* newspaper was laying in front of her door. She grabbed it and took it to the restaurant. On the front page of the paper was the headline, "Police Chiefs invade Phoenix." As she read the story, she burst out laughing when she read, "You can tell the Police Chiefs from the residents because they will be the ones who aren't armed."

It was only a block and a half walk to the Convention Center. At every corner there were at least four uniformed cops. In front of the Center there were thirty marked cruisers from City, County and State Police agencies and she now understood that the show of force was to protect the attendees to the convention.

She registered at the desk and was told that her presentation was filled for all three of the sessions they had scheduled and would she be willing to do a fourth? She looked at the IACP rep and said, "Of Course." The rep laughed and said that the only times they have gotten this kind of response was for firearm classes and they hoped she was prepared for a lot of questions. The rep provided her with an attendee list for the three programs which showed cops from all over the U.S. and several foreign countries scheduled to attend.

Rather than roam around the vendor area of the Convention Center, Lissa went back to her hotel room to prep for the ninety-minute presentation. She started with the fact that she had been the victim of sexual assault and that, even though the police were supportive of her, they were neither trained or prepared for the physical and mental trauma. Using Marty, she showed how the advocate attended every court appearance. Then she told about the child psychologist meeting with the victim at least twice per week while the adult psychologist met with the mother. And she said that she was surprised that when the case had been successfully prosecuted and the father sentenced to life, that the mental health professionals volunteered to continue their counselling for as long as necessary, while still continuing to get assignments with their team. She added into the presentation the fact that the other disciplines showed excitement at being incorporated into the criminal justice process.

The one hundred chairs in the room were all occupied for each of the four presentations. Lissa wished that she had videotaped some of the meetings of the teams or had some form of visual presentation, but it was clear that the room full of people were hanging on her every word. At the conclusion of each of the sessions, she received a standing ovation from a room full of her brothers and sisters in blue. She was mobbed by people asking questions and enlisting her help in setting up a program in their community. She found it to be a very humbling experience.

On the final day of the conference Lissa received a text from Liza saying she needed to call her immediately. Lissa called Liza's cell phone and there was a pause and it sounded like Liza's voice was cracking. Liza told Lissa that Sheba was in the living room and took a step and collapsed. Liza took Sheba to the veterinarian who determined that Sheba had cancer which would require the removal of the leg. The vet also said that the diagnosis was terminal as the cancer had spread throughout the dog's body. The vet's recommendation was that Sheba be put down because the dog would only suffer more and more each day. Lissa fell back onto the bed and tried to get her breath back. Her best friend in the world was dying and the decision on when she would die was Lissa's to make. Lissa told Liza to give her a few minutes and she would call back.

Lissa sat on the bed and cried her eyes out. She knew that putting the dog down was the right thing to do, but the selfish part of her did not want to lose her BFF. She pulled herself together and made the dreaded call to go ahead and end Sheba's life. Lissa spent the entire plane flight back to Cincinnati in a stupor that was so obvious that the flight attendants asked her if she needed a doctor. They were concerned because the flight manifest indicated that she was an armed law enforcement officer. The drive home was no better.

Liza was at the door when Lissa opened it. They hugged and cried. Liza said that Sheba was administered a drug to sleep and that Sheba looked at her with tired eyes and placed her head on Liza's leg. The second drug was administered and Sheba quietly gasped out her last breath. Liza dragged Lissa over to a mantel that held a vase. The vase had an inscription below Sheba's picture which said simply, "A TRUE CHAMPION." Liza handed Lissa the vet bill, but said, "The vase is my gift to a great friend.

CHAPTER TWENTY

Lissa threw every effort into her new assignment. On her first day back to work she found that she was being transferred to the Training Unit as Commander of the Police Academy.

Her first action was to call a meeting of all of the instructors assigned to the Training Unit. She told them in clear and uncertain terms that, "You have an obligation to live up to the sign hanging above the classroom door. Your only function is to make our officers the best in the world. You will do that by being properly prepared for every class you teach, by encouraging questions and by treating students with the respect they deserve. Just like them, you started knowing little and your instructors made you what you are today. I will not tolerate anything less than excellence from you and from them."

She had been in the position less than three months when the announcement of a test for the position of Captain was released. She decided to take a week vacation and went to Nashville, Indiana, a small resort town seventy miles west of Cincinnati, to study for the test. When the test scores came out, Lissa sat atop the list of thirty-five who took it. She walked out into the cool Cincinnati evening air outside of the training center and looked into the sky and said, "That was for you Sheba!"

While she waited for her promotion to come through, she prepared for a new recruit class to begin their training. She walked into the class of sixty men and women who were standing at attention for her arrival dressed in crisp recruit gray uniforms. She looked at the class and told them to be seated. She began her presentation with:

"My name is Lieut. Harding and I am the Commander of the Cincinnati Police Academy. All of the people you will see standing up here instructing you, with just a few exceptions, once sat in the same chairs you sit in today. After graduating college, I came to Cincinnati and found a security guard job at a retail corporate headquarters while
I searched for a position as a police officer. I joined the
Cincinnati Police Department after working for the Kentucky Attorney General as an investigator and made my way up the ranks though hard work and dedication to this agency. You will also have that opportunity.

"When I arrived at this position, I met with all of the instructors and ordered them to make you, as the sign above the entrance says, the best police officers in the country. People can argue as to whether NYPD or LAPD is the finest police agency in the U.S., but you will not be serving in those cities. We want you to be the best to the residents of Cincinnati, Ohio, nothing more, nothing less.   "If you ask one hundred cops what it means to protect and serve, you will get the same answer as to what it means to protect. They will all say that it is their sworn duty to protect people from predators looking to prey on them. The same one hundred cops will each give a different answer to what it means to serve. Let me give you my definition. Serving the citizens of this City means that you will treat them with respect and dignity; you will treat them fairly and with compassion. You will answer their calls for service and provide whatever assistance you can, and you will professionally represent the storied history of the Cincinnati Police Department at all times.

"Your instructors are here to help you accomplish that goal. They will be available to you to answer your questions and their door will always be open to you. If you find a door that is not open, all you need to do is tell me and I will assure you that the door will open. The instructors know that their function is to help you become successful police officers and I will tolerate nothing less.

"As you begin this journey, I commit to you that you will never walk alone. Good Luck!"

CHAPTER TWENTY-ONE

Her promotion to Police Captain was held in City Council chambers with television crews from all of the local stations in attendance. She saw herself on the evening news shaking hands with the Police Chief and the three Assistant Chiefs. She was told that she would be the
Commander of District Four replacing another female Captain who was being moved to oversee the Operations Division.

Lissa arrived at the District for her first day as a Captain. The desk officer jumped out of his chair to salute her. She returned the salute and walked back to her new office where she was greeted by Lieutenant Dave Humbard, the Executive Officer. Humbard welcomed her to the District and told Lissa, "My transfer request is on top of your desk. It is not that I want a transfer, but it is protocol to offer in case you want someone else as your Exec." Lissa did not say a word. She just walked back to her desk and picked up the transfer. Dropping it into the shredder she said, "Just make me look good and we will get along famously."

She told Humbard to set up a meeting with all of the Lieutenants for the following day at eight a.m., telling him "This is a mandatory meeting. The only excusable absence is that they are dead. I also want to meet with every community council over the next two weeks." Humbard was writing feverishly to impress the new Captain because he liked his Monday through Friday day-shift job.

Humbard showed her how to change the password protection on her computer and then left her alone in the office. Lissa made her password shebawillalwaysbemyhero". She sat at the big desk and looked at the wall which had a map with colored pins mapping the crime in the District. She wrote a note to have Humbard explain to her what the different colors represented, so that she would have an idea on effective ways of reducing activity in areas with a lot of pins.

The morning went by quickly and she needed to be at District One for an afternoon staff meeting with the Police Chief. All of the Captains and Assistant Chiefs were present in the conference room and she was welcomed into the Administrative staff of the Cincinnati Police Department.

She went home after the staff meeting and laid down on the couch to take a nap. At nine-thirty she dressed and went back to the District. The desk officer was shocked to see the Captain at ten p.m., but Lissa put her finger over her lips to indicate he should remain silent and walked down the hall to the Supervisors Office. She threw open the door and yelled, "Get off your dead ass and salute your new boss, you old fart!" Sgt. Woodson slowly got up from the chair that his body completely filled and moved his right arm upward in a deliberate motion usually reserved for police funerals to salute Lissa. She ran over and hugged him whispering, "You are a major reason why I am wearing these railroad tracks and I wanted to thank you personally."

He looked at her and asked, "Are you planning to address the roll call Captain?" She nodded her head and he said, "Fine, wait by the door and I will prep them for you." The two walked to the briefing room and the Sergeant walked in alone. He looked at the cops who appeared to have not had their coffee yet and yelled, "A-TEN'HUT!" The cops jumped to attention and Lissa walked into the room, saluting all of the cops getting ready for third shift.

She said, "I am Captain Harding and I am the new Commander of District Four. I just wanted to introduce myself and say a few words. I will be meeting with all of the Lieutenants tomorrow morning and I will be telling them that I will hold them responsible for your screw-ups, so if you want to see their balls hanging from the flagpole outside, here is your chance. We are going to give the citizens of this District their money's worth by providing the best possible service. If you are not prepared to buy into that, put a transfer request on my desk and I will immediately sign it. Have a safe night and go home to those you love." With that she saluted Sergeant Woodson and left the room.

There were seven Lieutenants in the conference room when she arrived. She sat at the head of the table and checked out the fact that each of them was looking quizzically at her wondering what she was going to say. She opened by introducing herself and then said, "Here is the deal.

I intend to hold each of you individually accountable for the actions of the people who work under you. I told third shift last night that, if they screw-up, it will be your testicles hanging from the flagpole outside of this building. And I expect you to tell the Sergeants that work under you the exact same thing. This WILL be the best District in the City or I will have a new supervisory staff. If you have a problem with that, simply request a transfer. Without taking a single question, she got out of her chair and left the room.

***

Lissa got a call from Robin Miller inviting her to a shindig at Kenwood Country Club. Robin said she was invited by a member and told to bring a guest. Lissa reluctantly agreed but said she would drive herself in case something happened in the District.

When she arrived in the front circle there was a valet to park her unmarked car and Robin was standing in the front entrance.

The two walked in and were directed to the second floor where there was a party room. The host, a former Cincinnati Vice cop, who owned his own private investigation service, was waiting at the door. When the three walked into the room, Lissa saw a banner with read, 'WELCOME CAPTAIN HARDING!" In the room were cops from C.I.S., the medical people from the Sexual Assault Teams, and supervisors and cops from the Districts that Lissa had worked in. In all there were sixty-seven people in attendance. The partiers were served a great dinner, then drinks and a DJ had been hired to play for them.

Robin refused to let Lissa's glass get empty and she was really tipsy as the evening progressed. She knew that she would be unable to drive her City car in her condition, but the Security Director for the club, who was a retired cop, told her he would drive her car to her home and have another employee follow to take him back to the club. Whether it was the alcohol she consumed or just a need for companionship, Lissa began dancing and talking with a Psychologist from University Medical Center and he offered to take her home. The three-car caravan made the fifteen minute drive to Lissa's house and her cruiser was parked in her driveway. She handed the Security Director two twenty dollar bills as a tip, but he handed one back and told her he didn't work for tips but the other guy did.

Lissa invited the Doctor in for a nightcap and he accepted. Dr. Tyne was a fifty-one-year-old divorcee and was a marathon runner with a hot body. As they sipped on their scotch, he grabbed Lissa and gave her a long and passionate kiss. The kiss progressed until she grabbed him by the hand and pulled him into her bedroom. They undressed each other and Lissa felt a wetness that she had not felt in years. They fell onto the bed and Lissa whispered that he could not explode inside her.

Lissa mounted him and slowly let him fill her. As he went deeper inside her, the tingle became more intense. Lissa was unsure she would be able to envelop all of him as he was very well endowed. When she finally felt his skin meet hers, his erection hit her cervix and she felt a shot of pain. She didn't move until the pain subsided, then began rocking back and forth slowly. As the sensation she was feeling intensified, so did her gyrations. She was slapping against his body until she felt the full release of her orgasm. She could see by his face that he was also ready to explode so she slid off of him while still getting aftershocks. She decided that this was the right time to actually taste semen and she placed her mouth around the head and then slid him deeper into her mouth trying to get all of him. She heard a moan and then felt the explosion which caused her to gag as his juices went deep into her throat. The taste was a bit salty and she could feel the head of his penis expanding with each pulsation as he was being drained. The two sprawled out on the bed and went to sleep.

When the alarm sounded, the doctor was already in the shower. When he came out Lissa showered and dressed for work. Not a word was exchanged until the two walked out the door and Lissa said, "Thanks for the ride!" There was a wry smile on the doctor's face as he said, "You are very welcome." They both knew that this was a one-time event not likely to ever be repeated.

CHAPTER TWENTY-TWO

Lissa spent the next two weeks meeting with the sixteen community councils that are in District Four and told each the same thing. She said, "We are here to serve your needs and we will work diligently to achieve that goal. I will make myself available to your leaders, but there is something that you need to fully understand. Just because you are seeing immediate results to whatever the issue is, does not mean that we are not addressing it. Take for example a gang or drug sales issue. It may take us months of work to make criminal charges that will result in convictions. And we cannot risk compromising our work by keeping you updated on who we are investigating and how it is progressing. Rest assured that we do take your complaints seriously and do everything possible to address them."

Lissa decided to start having her lunch with the shift supervisors. She would grab whoever was in the District and drive them to lunch. Somewhere along the way she would pull her unmarked car over and play a game called "what if?" She would pull up in front of an office building and say there was a report of two men burglarizing the second floor. How would the supervisors deploy personnel? Or pull up to a large warehouse and tell the supervisors that there was a large fire with hazardous materials and want to know how they would secure the streets and deal with the residents and businesses.

After the first week, she was having trouble finding any supervisors in the District at or near lunch time.

Lissa was sitting in her office working on mapping crime in the southern portion of the District where there had been a spike in violent crime when the door burst open and her Exec ran in. He said, "Captain, there is a young woman at the front desk demanding to see you about a personal matter and she refuses to tell us what it is about."

Without looking up from her work, Lissa said simply, "bring her on back." A couple of minutes later he returned with a tall blonde haired woman who appeared to be in her late teens. Lissa stood up and extended her hand saying, "I am Captain Harding, please have a seat." Lissa asked Dave, "Would you please get me a coffee and the young lady a soft drink and close the door behind you." She looked at the young woman and said, "I have to tell you that I am a bit confused. I was told that you have an urgent personal matter. Can you help clarify that for me?"

The girl stared directly into Lissa's eyes and said, "My name is Debra Dewarcs. I am nineteen and a sophomore at Ohio State University. Just recently my parents informed me that I was adopted at birth and I wanted to find my birth parents. My parents told me that they never actually met my birth mother and that I was not given a name at birth. They said that I was born on September eleventh at Christ Hospital and they paid for me to come to Cincinnati on a bus and my hotel room so that I could track down the information. The only "Jane Doe" listed on a birth certificate on that day showed the mother to be Melissa Harding and the father as unknown. I searched the name on the Internet and came up with you."

She had just finished speaking when Dave opened the door and handed her a Diet Pepsi and placed the Captain's coffee on her desk. He could read the look of disbelief on the Captain's face that something was wrong, but Lissa said, "Thank you Dave. That will be all. Please make sure that I am not disturbed." Lissa continued, "Debra, I do not know whether or not I am your birth mother, but I have the resources to get you a definitive answer. I did give birth to a girl on that date and I did not give her a name to allow the adopting parents to develop a bond with their new baby. As for the lack of a father's name, I was raped and became pregnant. He has spent the last nineteen years rotting in a cell in an Ohio prison."

With that, she picked up the telephone and called the Hamilton County Coroner's Office saying, "This is Captain Harding of Cincinnati District Four. I would like to speak to the Coroner." When she was connected, she said, "Doctor, I need a favor. I need to get an expedited paternity test done. It does not involve a criminal matter, so I will pay whatever it costs, but I need the results by tomorrow." The Coroner told her that it would cost two thousand dollars for that kind of expedited service and that, if the samples reached the Coroner's Office by the end of the business day, she would have the results the next day. Lissa told the Coroner that the samples would arrive at their office within the hour.

Lissa hung up and walked down the hall to the investigators office and asked for two swabs for DNA. She was given two glass containers and she returned to her office. After closing the door, she opened the first container and swabbed the inside of her own cheek, carefully placing the swab in the glass vial and sealing it.

She looked at Debra and said, "Please open your mouth so that I can get a swab of your DNA to match against mine." Debra opened her mouth and that damp swab was sealed in a different container. Lissa placed both containers in an evidence bag and sealed it. She walked out her door and said, "Dave, have a beat car handdeliver this directly to the County Coroner. I promised that it would be there within the hour." Although now totally confused, the Lieutenant ran to the desk and found a cop to deliver the package.

Lissa returned to her office and asked, "How did you get here today?" Debra answered, "By bus." Lissa said, "Since it appears that I might be your birth mother, let's check you out of your hotel. You can stay at my house and we will find out together. It will also save your parents some money." The two left the office with Lissa telling the Exec, "You can reach me on my cell phone if you need me."

They drove to the Cincinnatian Hotel and checked Debra out, then drove to Lissa's home. When they pulled into the driveway Lissa noticed a large box outside her front door. Not expecting any deliveries, Lissa told Debra to wait by the car until the package could be identified. On the top of the box was a card that read, "FROM YOUR FRIENDS AT THE CANINE UNIT. SHE NEEDS A LOVE ONLY YOU CAN GIVE." Lissa pulled on the box. It lifted right up showing a crate containing a jet black German Shepard puppy who appeared to be about twelve weeks old.

Tears began flowing down Lissa's cheeks and Debra ran over asking, "What is happening?" Lissa softly said, "My canine was shot in the line of duty. She survived and became a pet until she contracted cancer and had to be put down about two years ago. She was the best friend I ever had. This puppy was delivered to me by the cops in the canine unit of the police department."

Lissa carried the crate into the house and Debra carried the empty box. Lissa set the crate in the center of the living room and took Debra to the spare bedroom. After changing out of her uniform, Lissa opened the crate and the female puppy bounced around the living room, jumping in and out of Lissa's lap and incessantly licking her face. Lissa crawled over to a corner and grabbed a green tennis ball that belonged to Sheba. She rolled the ball and she and Debra rolled in laughter as the puppy attacked the ball. The puppy tried to control the tennis ball with her front paws, but ended up rolling around without gaining any control.

Lissa told Debra that there was a restaurant in Mount Lookout Square that had been featured on the Food Network for its hamburgers and that they could get the puppy a burger as well. They took the slow walk down the tree lined street with neatly mown lawns. It was a beautiful early evening in Cincinnati. They were seated in a booth in a corner looking out on the bustling corner. Lissa asked, "What would you like to drink Debra?" Debra said, "My parents let me drink alcohol, so I would really like a beer." Lissa started to tell her that Ohio law prohibits serving a minor, but remembered that there is an exception if a parent orders and serves the alcohol to the minor. Believing that she actually was the girl's mother, when the waiter asked what they would like to drink, Lissa said, "We will have a whiskey sour and a Miller Lite." The waiter looked at Debra and said, "I will need to see her ID." Lissa reached into her purse and fished out her badge and identification. She flashed her Captain's badge and said, "This is my daughter and I will serve it to her." The young waiter looked intently at the badge and said, "I will be right back." He went to a manager and asked him what to do. The manager walked over to the table and said, "This is your daughter, Captain, and you are going to give her the beer?" Lissa nodded yes and the manager looked at the waiter and said, "Get them their drinks."

They looked at the menu which offered multiple types of burgers and then ordered. While Debra sipped on her beer, Lissa said, "You seem to know a lot about me, but I don't know anything about you. Why don't you tell me about yourself?"

Debra said, "My parents told me that they left Cincinnati within a month after they adopted me. My dad is a paramedic with the Canton Fire Department and is ready to retire. My mother is an Emergency Room nurse at a hospital in Canton. My parents have loved me all of my life and tried to give me everything I could want or need. I played volleyball and basketball in high school and they made my games whenever they could because of their crazy schedules. I am a Pharmacology major at OSU.

My parents told me they tried for five years to conceive a child, but my dad's sperm count was so low that they could not give him medication to bring it up. They saved for those five years for their child's education and had enough money to pay for my college expenses. I have really had a great life. Can I ask you a question now? I am really curious as to why you would give up a baby you carried for nine months." Lissa thought for a second and answered, "My baby was not conceived out of love, it was the result of a sexual assault. I did not believe that I would be able to offer the love to that child and wanted her to have a full life with the love of parents."

The two sat and talked for hours and then walked back to Lissa's house where they went to sleep. Lissa reached under her bed where she kept Sheba's bed and retrieved the puppy who she named Cybil Shepard after the movie star. She placed the dog in the bed which was placed in the same place that Sheba had slept.

Lissa was just getting out of the shower when her cell phone rang. It was the Coroner who asked, "I have the results. Do you want me to tell you over the phone?" Lissa immediately said, "No, place the results in an envelope and leave it at the front desk for me. I will drop the check off for the full amount. I owe you."

Lissa told Debra that they needed to go to the lab to pick up the results. She went back to the bedroom and wrote the check and they left after putting Cybil back in her crate.

When Lissa came out of the lab with the envelope, she handed it to Debra and said, "I have no clue what it says. This is your search, so it's only fair that you read the results first. Debra ripped open the letter and read it without saying a word. Lissa waited patiently when Debra blurted out, "You are my birth mother!" Lissa said, "Let's stop for breakfast before I drop you off at the bus station for your trip home. If it is okay with your parents and you would like to come back for the summer vacation, I would love to have you spend some time here." The two hugged at the bus station and there were visible tears.

Lissa's last words were, "If you need anything, call me immediately." Your parents are lucky to have a daughter like you."

Each Captain in Cincinnati takes a turn as Night Chief. They work from eight at night until four in the morning to handle any overnight emergency. Lissa had spent most of the first four days of her rotation inside District Four formulating a plan to deal with a pocket of gang violence in a neighborhood near the University of Cincinnati. She was getting dreary eyed at one a.m. on Friday night and decided to head toward downtown where there would be people wandering the streets prior to bar closing at two-thirty.

She was headed downtown when her cell phone rang. It was police communications advising her that an officer had been seriously injured in a headon crash with a drunk driver on Fort Washington Way, a limited access connector between I75 and I-71. Lissa jammed the portable blue and red strobe into the dashboard and turned on the siren screaming toward the crash.

Units had the road completely closed off, but Lissa drove around the barricade and pulled up just short of the two mangled vehicles. Firemen were working feverishly to remove the roof of the police car, as the damage had made it impossible to get into the car to help the driver. Lissa walked up to an officer standing and watching and asked, "Who is the officer in the car?" The cop looked at her and said, "Officer Seemoan, Captain."

Lissa gasped for air and forced herself to take a slow deep breath to clear her mind. She asked the officer where the driver of the other car was and he pointed toward a police cruiser behind the crash scene.

Lissa walked over to the car where two officers were standing. She asked if the suspect was injured and one sarcastically said, "Of course not. The sonofabitch refused medical aid. He has also demanded an attorney." Lissa looked at the two cops and said, "This is what is going to happen. You will take him to C.I.S. and tell whoever is there to drag a judge out of bed and get a search warrant to draw his blood. One of you will be with him every minute. If he needs to shit, one of you will watch him do it. When you have the warrant in hand, take him to University Medical Center and get the blood drawn. I will have the Traffic Unit sign Aggravated Vehicular Assault and you will take him to the Justice Center. He is not to get there before four a.m. so that he cannot make the docket for this morning's court. That will give us twenty-four more hours to build our case. When he is booked, take the blood to the lab and tell them it is a rush. We will not charge him with Operating a Vehicle Under the Influence (OMVI) until we have the blood results."

Liza was loaded into the paramedic unit and taken to University Medical, a Level One trauma center with a lead and following police escort. All the paramedics would tell Lissa was that Liza was unconscious, but breathing on her own. Lissa telephoned the Chief to advise him of the situation and then drove to University Medical Center.

When she arrived, she could see the line of Media trucks parked out front. When she got out of her cruiser, they ran toward her like she was Hillary Clinton sneaking out of an event. Lissa waited until all four local stations had microphones in her face and said, "My name is Captain Harding and I will give you a brief statement of the events as we know them at this moment. At the conclusion, there will be no questions. At approximately 1:20 a.m. a vehicle traveling the wrong way on Fort Washington Way struck a marked Cincinnati Police car head-on. The injured officer was brought here by Cincinnati Fire Paramedics and is currently being treated for what are believed to be lifethreatening injuries.   The suspect, who we are not identifying at this time, was taken to the Hamilton County Justice Center and being charged with Aggravated Vehicular Assault. He refused medical aid at the scene.
That is all I have for you.

As the media maniacs screamed questions, Lissa turned her back on them and walked into the hospital. She went directly to the Emergency Room and was told by the doctor that Lissa had suffered serious back injuries and may have severed her spine. He said that they had sent her to surgery and that they might have more information. The area around the ER was filling with uniformed cops, all of whom were demanding information about how the officer was doing. Lissa told the cops to go to the fifthfloor surgery waiting room and, as soon as she had some definitive information, she would update them. The Police Chief arrived and Lissa briefed him on what had transpired so far.

After more than five hours of waiting, Lissa was beginning to get really weary. The Police Chief took one look at her and said, "Go home Lissa. I will call you as soon as I know anything. That is not a request. That is an order." The Chief looked at the room full of cops and said, "Who is here on my dime with a marked cruiser?" Four cops raised their hands. The Chief pointed out two of them and said, "One of you drive the Captain's car to her house and the other follow and then return here."

When Lissa got home, she took off her uniform and took Cybil out for a potty break. She went back inside and collapsed on the couch with her cell phone inches from her head. Cybil pawed on the couch until Lissa picked her up and placed her in a comfy place in the small of her back. They both were asleep within seconds. Two hours later the cell rang and Cybil grumbled from the jolt of Lissa jumping up to answer it.

The Chief told her that Liza was going to survive, but that she would be paralyzed from the waist down for life. The crash had severed the L3 vertebrae and there was nothing that doctors could do. He went on to praise the way Lissa handled the situation, but those words fell on deaf ears as Lissa was in a state of total shock. The Chief told her to stay home because Liza would be unavailable for visits until the next morning. Lissa hung up the phone and picked up Cybil taking her into the bedroom. Instead of putting Cybil in her dog bed, Lissa moved a pillow and placed the dog right next to her. Cybil was inches from Lissa's ear and she could hear the dog breathing as it fell asleep almost instantly. That breathing strangely had a calming effect on Lissa and she too fell asleep quickly.

Lissa arrived at the hospital just before nine in the morning. She went to the room where Liza was after stopping at the nurse's station for an update. She walked into the room and softly touched Liza's hand. Liza opened her eyes and looked directly into Lissa's eyes which told a story. Liza said, "How screwed am I?" Lissa hemmed and hawed saying, "You should get your medical status from a medical profession and that ain't me." Liza said, "Those assholes won't tell me anything. You are my friend and you OWE ME!" Lissa sighed and said, "It is unlikely you will ever be able to walk again. Other than that, you are a rock star. I need to get to work and you need to get your rest. I will be back soon."

Over the next two weeks, Lissa stopped in to see Liza every day. Liza was recovering the best she could and the doctors decided to move her to a rehabilitation facility called Drake Hospital which is located at the northern limit of the City. It is a long-term care center which specializes in catastrophic injuries.

***

Lissa appeared at the arraignment of the suspect, a man named Daniel Kong, who was represented by the highest priced D.U.I lawyer in Cincinnati.

The lawyer argued for a low bond because Mr. Kong was a prominent business owner and a lifelong resident of Cincinnati. Lissa jumped up and told the judge that the officer would likely never walk again and that the blood results were point one-eight-six, more than ten points over the legal limit in Ohio. Bond was set at two million dollars cash and Lissa was totally frustrated when Kong was freed less than two hours later.

Lissa called Tim Cusher to represent Liza's interests. Cusher gladly accepted the case and his research found that Kong had one million dollars in auto insurance and was worth in excess of ten million dollars. The insurance company settled almost immediately and Cusher filed a lawsuit on behalf of Liza for ten million more.

***

Lissa told Liza that she was making renovations on her house to make it wheelchair accessible and that Liza would be moving in with her. When Liza objected, Lissa said, "Shut the fuck up woman. This isn't up for negotiation."

Liza and the dog began to take its toll on Lissa. She was feeling stress and decided to make an appointment to see the department shrink who told her to take some of the time she accumulated and leave town. She and Cybil went to Cumberland Lake, where she had taken Sheba and the two played by the lake for four days before she went to Tennessee to see her parents. She told her parents about actually meeting her daughter and promised to try to get Debra down to Tennessee to meet them. She found out that her brother had suffered a severed finger while servicing a car, but that he was still able to do his job. The peace and serenity of Lafollette was just what the doctor ordered and, when they returned to Cincinnati, Lissa and Cybil were relaxed and refreshed.

Liza moved in with Lissa seven months later. With the renovations that Lissa had made, Liza was able to move around the house, into the yard, and even able to cook in the kitchen. Lissa found that Liza was an accomplished cook who made delicious gourmet food for them nightly. The insurance settlement allowed Liza to buy a specially equipped van with a remote entry so she could roll right up to the steering wheel without assistance. It had hand controls for breaking and acceleration as well. That made it possible for her to do grocery shopping with the help of the staff of the store. She was formally retired from the Police Department with a promotion to Police Specialist, the rank of Corporal in most police departments.

***

Lissa maintained contact with Debra and was thrilled when she told Lissa she would be coming to Cincinnati for the summer. Although room in the house would not be an issue, Lissa didn't know how Liza would impact the summer plans. Debra was amenable to meeting her biological grandparents and stopping by Lake Cumberland. Lissa told Debra that she would never be her parent, but that they could become lifelong friends.

Debra also took to Liza because of the intestinal fortitude that this woman in a wheelchair exhibited. She would go shopping with Liza while Lissa was working and they would play board games and play with Cybil in the back yard.

***

Lissa was sitting at her desk when the police radio screamed of an officer involved shooting in District Four.

The unit number was a plainclothes car. Lissa ran out the door and went to the scene in Code three mode. When she arrived she was shocked to see Robin Miller being treated by a paramedic. Miller had cuts and bruises on her face. Lissa ran over and said, "Robin, are you okay?" Robin said, "I had to shoot...", but Lissa stopped her in her tracks saying, "You requested an attorney, so I am not allowed to ask you any questions. Do not volunteer anything until you have legal counsel with you, do you understand?"

While the paramedics continued treating Robin, Lissa walked over to her partner and said, "What the fuck happened?" Her new partner had just gotten promoted to detective and said, "We came here looking for a suspect in a rape that occurred at U.C. I knocked on the front door, but when I turned around, Robin was nowhere to be found. I heard her scream around the back and then heard two shots.

When I got back there the suspect had taken two contact shots to the chest and was very dead."

The Chief arrived at that point and Lissa walked over to brief him on what she knew. She told the Chief that Det. Miller had invoked her right to counsel, so no questions were asked of her. She could see the Chief was unhappy with that knowledge, but she was going to make sure Robin was treated fairly.

Robin told two detectives from the Homicide Unit to transport Robin to the hospital to be checked out. She also told them, "I want close-up pictures of every abrasion, bruise or laceration on her body. I don't care if she has to get naked, I want ALL of her injuries documented."

Because the Chief was at the scene, Lissa did not have to deal with the media. The Chief told them that two detectives were attempting to locate a suspect in a sexual assault case and that there was an altercation in the rear yard of the residence with a female detective. The female fired two shots and the suspect was killed.   He told them the female officer had been transported to the hospital with minor injuries and that the investigation was in the very preliminary stages.

While the press conference was proceeding, Lissa called the F.O.P. headquarters and told them to have an attorney at the Homicide Unit to meet Det. Robin Miller who had been involved in a deadly force encounter. She also told the secretary who answered, "This call never happened. Got it?"

The case was turned over to the Hamilton County Prosecutor who, with the Police Chief, held a press conference announcing that the officer had a reasonable fear for her life and that the use of deadly force was within the law. Protestors outside the courthouse were visibly upset by the outcome and threatened violence with the infamous, "NO JUSTICE, NO PEACE" chant. The City was braced for violence, but a special contingent called "Cincinnati Initiative to Reduce Violence" was out in force calming the waters. The group is made up of former gang members and criminals who can speak the language and has the respect of the community.

CHAPTER TWENTY-FOUR

Lissa received a call from the Police Chief's secretary telling her that the Chief wanted her to come to his office. Lissa put down the report that showed her District had a twenty-seven percent reduction in violent crime in the past year and she hoped that her efforts would be recognized at this meeting.

When she arrived on the third floor of District One, the secretary told her the Chief was waiting for her and to go right in. The Chief pointed to a chair and Lissa sat down. The Chief said, "I am really impressed with the things you have accomplished since being assigned to District Four. I am creating an additional Assistant Chief position and would like you to consider the position. I have to tell you up front that this you will serve at my pleasure and, since you do not have the time or age to retire, might be a factor in your consideration. I need an answer within the next two days. That will be all."

Lissa went home and sat down with Liza to discuss the offer. Liza advised against taking the position because she could also be fired for no reason by the City Manager as well as the Police Chief. Liza told Lissa that this all came about in 2009 when voters in Cincinnati passed a change in the law to allow for the hiring of the Police Chief and the Assistant Chiefs without Civil Service testing, because the City wanted to hire its first African-American Police Chief. The City already knew who it wanted for the position and hired the Police Chief of Portland, Maine, who had spent twenty-six years with LAPD.

Lissa decided to pass the news that she would not be accepting the position in person. She walked into the outer office and the secretary beamed a smile and said, "The Chief has been expecting you. Go right in." Lissa sat down and looked into the eyes of the Chief and said, "Chief, I gave serious consideration to the offer and I truly appreciate being considered, but I am going to have to decline. There are still things I really want to accomplish at D4." She could tell by the scowl on the Chief's face that he was unhappy with her decision. The Chief gave her a hand motion that it was time for her to leave his office. Lissa had a gut feeling that there would be retaliation for her "snub" and she could not have been more accurate.

Three days after her meeting with the Chief, Lissa received her transfer orders. She would now be overseeing the property room and the supply unit. She would lose her take home car and would be taken out of the rotation of being Night Chief.

On her last day in District Four, Lieutenants, Sergeants, Investigators and beat cops dropped off flower arrangements and told Lissa how much she would be missed. Dave helped her box up the items in the office and then drove her home. There were tears in the twentyone year veteran cop's eyes as he told Lissa, "You were the best boss I ever had and you really got screwed." Lissa hugged Dave and wished him well and then walked into her house.

She had to drive her own car the fourteen miles to the Police Property Room, which is located in a renovated warehouse just west of downtown Cincinnati. The cop behind a screen gave her a code to enter the warehouse and showed her back to her new office, which Lissa swore was once a storage closet. She would be supervising ten police officers, the youngest of which was fifty years old. They wore gray shirts like the police academy recruits and baseball caps. Street cops called it the "Home for old and decrepit cops" and that description was fairly accurate.

Her staff couldn't chase a four year old more than ten feet.

Lissa knew immediately that she had been sentenced to the "penalty box" and she was going to hate this assignment. Her first official act was to order an inventory of all of the property and she could hear the grumbling through the paper thin walls of her office. It took the old farts almost two weeks to compile the information that she requested. She sat at her desk and reviewed the volumes of evidence that the Property Room held until she came across an entry that froze her in her tracks. The entry listed four hundred eighteen thousand dollars in US currency and a date of March 19, 1982. There was no criminal case number or name on the listing. Lissa went to the officer on duty and demanded to be shown the evidence. The sixtyyear-old cop shrugged his shoulders and walked back to a rear corner and pointed to a cardboard box. Lissa lifted the box off the shelf and saw currency stacked in piles. On the outside of the box was on the date it was seized.

She returned to her office and sat at the desk looking at the telephone that had not rung once in the time she had been there. She picked up the phone and called the Chief's secretary, telling her she needed to see the Chief about an important matter. The secretary sighed and said, "Captain, you do know that you are not exactly on the
Chief's good side, don't you?" Lissa laughed and said, "That doesn't change the need to talk to him." The secretary scheduled an appointment for the next day.

Lissa walked into the Chief's office carrying the cardboard box filled with money. She set it down on his desk and said, "There is four hundred eighteen thousand dollars in this box which is in our evidence room. It has no case number or who it was seized from." The Chief shrugged his shoulders and said, "I was a Captain in Columbus, Ohio when this was seized.

Why is it my problem? Call the Prosecutor's Office and let them deal with it." Lissa picked up the box and walked out of the office.

Lissa returned the box to its home for the past thirty-three years and went to her phone to call the Hamilton County Prosecutor. She told them about the find and they promised to send an investigator over immediately. Twenty minutes later, the elected Prosecutor and his Chief Investigator arrived to inspect the box. The Prosecutor signed for the evidence and left with it.

Less than one hour later Lissa's phone was ringing incessantly with requests from the media regarding money found in the evidence room. She had no idea how the media got their information, but told each caller to contact the Public Information Officer of the Police Department for information. Within an hour Lissa got a call from Lieutenant Dania Matino, the P.I.O., who asked, "Did I pee in your Wheaties or what? I don't know anything about this!" Lissa answered, "Neither do I. Ask the Chief how he wants to handle it. I sure as hell didn't tell the media and I don't know who did."

As Lissa pulled into her driveway, she was feeling totally frustrated for the first time in her police career. Liza had dinner on the table and the two sipped wine and ate. When they were done and Lissa was putting dishes in the sink, her home phone line rang. The woman caller said, "Please hold for Director Comey." Lissa waited and a male voice said, "This is James Comey, Director of the Federal Bureau of Investigation. We have been following your career since you made your presentation at the I.A.C.P. convention and I would like to offer you an adjunct instructor position at our Academy in Quantico. Do you think you would be interested?"

Lissa was taken aback that the Director of the FBI was actually on the phone with her. She said, "Of course I would be interested. Who wouldn't?" Comey then asked, "When can you fly into Washington, DC to meet with me? We will pay all of your expenses for the trip." Lissa said, "I have a ton of time on the books, I just need to get it approved." They set an appointment for the following Thursday to give her five days to get her time off approved.

***

Lissa flew into Reagan International Airport and was met by a 30ish blonde male agent who looked like he played college basketball somewhere. He took her carry-on bag and drove her to the hotel, waiting in the lobby for her to get checked-in to her room. He then drove her to the J. Edgar Hoover Building in downtown DC and got her past the security checkpoint at the door.   He pushed the button which took her to the Administrative Level of the building and said, "I will wait down here for you. That floor is totally restricted, even to agents."

Lissa got off the elevator which was guarded by two FBI Police officers, the uniform division of the FBI. One of the officers escorted her down a long hallway and pointed to the right at a double cherry wood door. Lissa opened the door and was greeted by a secretary, whose first question was, "What can I get you to drink Captain Harding? The Director will be with you in just a moment. He is really looking forward to meeting you."

Comey opened the discussion with, "This would be a sworn position as a Special Agent with the FBI. You would be assigned as an Adjunct Instructor teaching Sexual Assault Investigations to new agents and being sent out to teach local and state police. You would be put into our retirement system and vested after five years of service. The salary would be a cut in pay from what you are making now, but the position offers a challenging opportunity for you to impart your extensive knowledge of developing relationships with victims and apprehending perpetrators. You would need to relocate to somewhere near Quantico. We would also pay for relocation expenses and help you find a home. Does this sound like something that would interest you?" Lissa took a deep breath and said, "I could lock in my Ohio retirement until I turn fifty-two, so the pay cut would not have an impact. I enjoy being in front of people helping them understand what the victim is actually experiencing as I was once a victim of rape myself. I would need to give Cincinnati notice that I am leaving and find a place to live." Comey said, "We can house you at our Academy while you look if that would help."

The two shook on Lissa's new position and, as promised, the jock FBI agent was waiting patiently in the lobby for her. She went back to her hotel where the kid promised to be back in the morning to take her to the Airport. As he was leaving, he asked, "Did you decide to join up with us?" Lissa smiled broadly and nodded yes.

Lissa called her parents from her room and told them she was joining the FBI as an instructor and they told her they were thrilled for her. She next called Liza and gleefully told her the news. She told Liza that she would sell her the house at a reasonable price if she wanted it and that she and Cybil would be moving within a month.

***

Upon her return to Cincinnati, Lissa wrote a letter of resignation and delivered it personally to the Chief's office. The secretary asked if she wanted to hand it to the Chief, but Lissa said, "That isn't necessary, he will be glad to have it."

Lissa sat on her couch and thought about how lucky she had been with her career choice. Cincinnati Police had provided her with opportunities and skills that would carry her the rest of her life. She would miss the brotherhood that she had experienced, but relished the thoughts of the challenges ahead for her.

EPILOGUE

Melissa Harding worked for the FBI for the next four years.
She met and married a physician from Georgetown University
Medical Center and the two built a home with a spectacular
view overlooking the Potomac River. She is writing on a manual
to train sexual assault investigators.

Cybil lived seventeen years and was loved.

Liza Seemoan died six months after Melissa left Cincinnati. The
Coroner ruled the death a direct cause of the automobile crash
and the suspect was re-tried for Vehicular Manslaughter. He
was sentenced to sixteen years in prison.

The man who raped Melissa was stabbed to death in a prison
fight less than one month from the scheduled end of his
twenty-five year sentence. No one came to claim the body and
he was buried in a field in the rear of the London Correctional
Institution.

Donny, the ten year old boy whose uncle abused him, was the
Class Valedictorian for the graduating class of the Kentucky
State Police Academy on his twenty-second birthday. He told
the audience that all that he became was the direct result of an
investigator from the Attorney General's Office sitting on a
floor in a playroom getting him to deal with his feelings.

Robin Miller never returned to work after the shooting. She received a medical disability pension from the State of Ohio for Post Shooting Stress.

Mellissa never heard from her biological daughter again.

www.ingramcontent.com/pod-product-compliance
Lightning Source LLC
Chambersburg PA
CBHW070556120726
47909CB00007B/2362